# SIDEBARRED

# SIDEBARRED

EMMA CHASE

This book is a work of fiction. All names, characters, locations,
and incidents are products of the author's imagination. Any
resemblance to actual persons, living or dead, locales, or events is
entirely coincidental.

Editor: Amy Tannenbaum
Cover designer: Hang Le, By Hang Le

*This one's for you, dear readers.*

# CHAPTER ONE

*July*

I still don't use an alarm clock.

My internal clock is as dependable as ever, but I don't wake up at 5 a.m. like I used to—I get up even earlier. Because these days it's not a run or the thought of fresh coffee that gets me going in the morning.

It's her.

I sense Chelsea before my eyes open. The press of her hip against my leg, the feel of her long, delicate arm draped across my bare chest, the tickle of her breath along my collarbone, the scent of lilac in her hair. The promise of lazy kisses, soft moans, and tight, wet heat.

We've been married for about two years and there hasn't been a single morning when I didn't wake with a smile tugging at my lips. Not one fucking time. Because she's beside me—half on top of me—and the six little shits we love more than anything are tucked safely away upstairs. They're all really good sleepers. That's key.

Getting laid with six awake kids in the house can be a challenge. It takes planning, stealth. When moments of spontaneous opportunity strike, they're never without risk of discovery. They require awareness—attunement to the movements and sounds beyond the closed door. What the kids are doing, where they are—if they're going to interrupt us with any one of a thousand ridiculous but urgent questions.

It can be a pain in the ass—though I wouldn't trade it for the world, wouldn't change a single thing about the life we've made together.

But here, now, in this bed, in the still darkness of morning—it's different. We can move how we want, say what we want—fuck in any position or on any surface that we can think of.

Because this is our time.

In these moments we're not a defense lawyer and a part-time museum curator, we're not parents, we're just Jake and Chelsea. A man and a woman who are crazy about each other.

Without opening my eyes I slide out from under her arm and down the bed, taking the blankets with me as I go. Once in a while, she'll surprise me and wake up before I do. Those are fun mornings. There is no greater wake-up call in the history of the world than the sight of Chelsea Becker's thick auburn hair covering my crotch and her plump, pouty lips wrapped greedily around my dick.

But today, I have the upper hand—and that's fun, too. I flip to my stomach and push Chelsea's thin nightgown up over her hips, exposing her to my now open eyes. She doesn't wear underwear to bed—there's really no point; it'd be on the floor come morning anyway. Her pussy is pink and perfect—smooth and bare except for a tiny auburn landing strip that never fails to turn me way the hell on. I rub my nose against the dusting of hair and inhale. And her scent—fuck—that gets me going, too. Clean and warm, like honeysuckle.

Her leg shifts near my shoulder and she lets out a little sigh.

Then I lick her.

Slowly, firmly, deep between those waiting lips, before gently circling her clit with the tip of my tongue.

Her foot slides up, bracing against the bed, her leg bent at the knee—and that little sigh turns into a longer moan. I open my mouth and kiss her, my tongue still dragging up and down, tasting her growing slickness.

I fucking love that. How easily she gets wet. Sometimes she's drenched before I even touch her. Once I asked if she dreamed about me going down on her, if that was why she was always so ready. But she just blushed and wouldn't answer.

I spear her with my tongue now—gliding in and out—sucking gently on that plump bundle of nerves.

Her voice is husky with sleep and heat when she moans.

"Fuck me . . ."

I can't tell if it's an expletive or an order. Either one works for me.

I crawl back up, turning Chelsea to her side and settling in behind her. My hand glides up her stomach to pull the top of her thin-strapped nightgown down so I can cover her breast and rub my palm against the peaked nipple.

Chelsea's hand comes up behind my head, guiding me to her mouth for a slow, deep kiss. I release her breast, lift her leg, and nudge my hips forward—my pelvis pushing against her ass and my cock sliding between her legs, hard and hot and searching. Chelsea breaks the kiss, turns her face toward the pillow, and pushes her hips back against me—telling me without words that she wants it and she wants it now.

I grip myself at the base and drag the head of my cock through her wet folds—rubbing against her clit, teasing her hole. My little wife whimpers, then she digs her fingernails into my thigh. "Jake . . ."

A chuckle rumbles behind my lips. Looks like teasing isn't on the menu today. This also works for me. I line myself up and thrust hard inside her—deep to the hilt.

Damn that's good. *So, so good.*

Chelsea's back bows and she breathes out a welcoming groan. I lift her leg and start pumping in and out—smooth, shallow, building jabs. Her inner muscles squeeze me fantastically, while the rest of her body goes slack with pleasure, her spine relaxing back against my chest.

I kiss her shoulder and lick her neck and bury my face in the waves of her silky hair. The sounds of our pants and slapping skin fill the air and our bodies grow slick with exertion—her pushing back against me as I withdraw and stroke up into her. And time stands still. Or more—it loses meaning. All that we know, all that matters, is the growing, electric pleasure coursing through us, sparking between us.

Making love sweetly has its place; long hours of endless foreplay are great, too. Hell, I can even get into the romance stuff—candles and rose petals and warm baths. But hard, fast fucking should never, ever be underestimated—'cause it's awesome. Even for married people, even for couples with kids.

Maybe especially for them.

There's something primal about giving into this base need—being rough and dirty and fast. There's something so intimate and comfortable and fucking honest about just wanting to come, and come hard, with the person you love.

It's a feeling I've only ever known with this woman in my arms—something I'll only ever share with her. *Till death do us part.*

"Please, Jake, please, please, please . . ." Chelsea chants mindlessly, and I know she's right on the edge. I let go of her leg and bring my hand to the juncture of her thighs—rubbing her clit in feather-light circles—providing the added pressure she needs.

She lifts her head and gasps when she comes, every muscle contracting and squeezing. My breaths are harsh and my hips push without a rhythm, until I roll us over so Chelsea's flat on her stomach and I cover her back. I thrust into her once, twice, and then my vision goes hazy as I come—the feeling so intense, all I can hear is the pounding of blood in my ears.

Damn.

Seconds, minutes, later we recover our breaths. I roll onto my back and wipe the sweat from my forehead with my arm. Chelsea rises up on her elbows and looks at me with sparkling blue eyes.

"Good morning."

I kiss her lips gently—because she's so fucking pretty. Because she makes me so stupidly happy.

"*Good* is an understatement."

I open my arms and she curls against me, giggling. We stay like that for only a few minutes because now it's a little after five—time to officially start my day. As usual, Chelsea drifts back to sleep as I kiss her forehead, ease out of bed, and get dressed for my morning run.

———

"I'm not gonna make it."

"Yes, you are."

"I'm gonna die."

"No, you're not."

She starts to sing, "If I die—"

"Stop quoting frigging country songs, Rosaleen. You're not dying."

*Frigging* isn't typically part of my vocabulary, but after a conversation with Chelsea—*several* conversations—and a few unfortunate imitations in preschool by Ronan, I'm making a concerted effort to tone down my language.

My running partner for the last two weeks, Rosaleen, gasps for breath as she jogs beside me, blond curly pigtails bouncing in the wind. She's eleven now. I can't fucking believe how fast she's changed from the little blond Shirley Temple look-alike I first met, who thought thirty was *so old*.

Well . . . she probably still thinks thirty is old, and thirty-four must be goddamn ancient.

Anyway, she's still short, still has those corkscrew curls and big, innocent blue eyes. But she's grown, changed—matured. A few months ago she started worrying about her weight, because she'd put on a little.

She also started wearing a training bra.

*So not going there.*

Chelsea explained it's just her age—that she'd arrived at the "awkward stage" and in a few months she'd hit a growth spurt and that extra weight would disperse the way it's supposed to. But Rosaleen didn't want to wait. So after I run seven miles on my own, I circle back and do an extra mile with her. She's improved—her running form and her stamina. Though you wouldn't know it by listening to her.

"After I'm gone . . . give Regan . . . my iPad."

I can't help but laugh as we turn the corner onto our street.

"Come on—there's the house," I coach. "Dig deep and get there."

Labored breathing is the only response I get.

I'm not the kind of guy who sings. Like—ever.

*Almost* ever.

The exception being when the kid beside me plucked my man-card from my death grip years ago—and pathetically begged for a lullaby while suffering a stomach virus.

And I caved. Spectacularly. With a One Direction ballad.

Humiliating? Sure. But since the damage has already been done . . .

"Da na nanana na na na nanana. Da na nanana na na na nanana. Da na nanana . . . nananana."

It's the *Rocky* theme song in case you can't tell. If you ever need an inspiration boost when working out? The *Rocky* sound track kicks ass.

"Da na naaaa, da na naaaaa!"

She laughs.

But damn if she doesn't pick up the pace.

"Da na naaaaaa, da na naaaaaa! Gonna fly now . . ."

Rosaleen crosses the threshold of the house, arms raised like a mini–Rocky Balboa at the top of the Philadelphia steps.

And seeing the pride on her face?

Humiliation's got nothing on that.

Once inside, Rosaleen immediately crumples to the living-room floor in a comatose heap. And stays there.

I grab two bottles of water from the kitchen, drink one myself, and put the other in her hand. "You want to come downstairs and lift weights with me?"

"Numph."

I pat the back of her head.

"Next week, then."

After lifting weights in the basement and a quick shower I head to the kitchen, where I'm greeted by chaos. Noisy, vibrating, bickering, laughing chaos.

Because the gang's all up, eating breakfast at the kitchen table.

"Can I have some more bacon?" Rory asks with his mouth full of scrambled eggs, his brown wavy hair falling over his forehead as he hunkers over his plate.

When I first met Rory McQuaid he was a pissed-off, stubborn little punk who was picking pockets and stealing cars to deal with the anger and devastation over his parents' sudden death. He's better now. Happier. Still a smart-ass, still gets a kick out of torturing his siblings, but he's steering clear of activities that could land him in juvenile detention.

"God, that's like your third serving," eighteen-year-old Riley complains. "Just eat the whole pound, why don't you?"

Rory and his twin brother, Raymond, are thirteen-year-old, growing boys—emphasis on *growing*. Either one waking up a quarter inch taller—and half a shoe size bigger—than they were the night before is fairly common. And like bats, they pretty much eat their weight in food.

Rory opens his mouth wide, flashing his sister the half-chewed horror on his tongue.

"You're so gross!"

"I'd rather be gross than a nag!"

Riley flings a piece of toast like a ninja star.

Before Rory can retaliate, Chelsea gives them The Look, then hands Rory three more pieces of bacon. I pour a cup of black coffee at the counter, turn around, and almost trip over tiny Regan, standing next to me with a hairbrush and elastic tie in her hand.

"Can you do my braid, Daddy?"

Regan and Ronan are the only two who call me and Chelsea "Mom" and "Dad"—too young to have any real memories of their parents, Robert and Rachel. To some, it might seem weird that the kids call us different names, but for us, it works.

I run the brush through her hair—it's getting really long—and weave the light-brown strands into a French braid in record time. She smiles, her top two teeth adorably missing, then sits at the table to finish her eggs.

On my right, I catch Chelsea giving me a different look than the one she tossed the kids' way. It's of the I-want-to-drop-to-my-knees-and-blow-you-so-bad variety.

"What?"

She shakes her head and steps closer. Her perfect breasts jiggle just a little beneath the lettering of her black San Diego Chargers jersey—and I lick my lips. I should've given her tits more attention this morning. I mentally promise to make it up to them tomorrow.

Chelsea's voice is low, so the kids can't hear. "There will never be anything sexier than watching you—with your muscles and tattoos—braiding a six-year-old's hair."

I shrug. "My braids are awesome."

"They are." She laughs. "And I love you."

"I love you, too." I lean down and kiss her.

Until Rory complains. "That's enough face sucking. You're *married* for God's sakes—act like it."

Chelsea giggles against my lips. But then whispers, "We should talk later."

Huh. She wants to talk. Great. Cool.

Said no guy ever.

"Everything okay?"

"Yeah. I think so. Just . . . later." She gives my forearm a squeeze—right over the tattoo with her and all the kids' names on it—and walks to the table to replenish the eggs.

I sit down at the head of the table, snag a piece of whole-wheat toast, and ask, "What are the plans for today, team?"

Riley pipes up first. "I'm going to Peter's."

Peter Wentworth is Riley's boyfriend of the last six months. He seems like a decent kid—doesn't piss his pants in my presence, like some of her past suitors. So I give him points for bravery. But . . . he's just such a fucking *dork*. A cosplaying, World of Warcraft–obsessed, could-be-an-understudy-for–*The Big Bang Theory* dork. Even for puppy love, I just don't think Peter's good enough for her.

Raymond raises his hand. "I have to go to the library to meet my group to finish a summer project for astronomy."

Rosaleen goes next. "I have piano."

Then Rory. "I have baseball practice."

And Regan. "I have ballet and tap today."

Then, finally, Ronan, his sandy-blond hair sticking up because no one's gotten around to brushing it for him. "I got nuffin."

I point my finger. "Then you're with me today, kiddo."

Chelsea sits down at the other end of the table.

"You're going to see the Judge?"

I nod. "I'll take Ronan with me, drop Rory at practice on the way, and pick him up on the way back."

"Rosaleen can come with me to Regan's dance class," Chelsea says. "We'll make it back home in time for her piano lesson." She turns to Riley. "And you can drop Raymond off at the library when you go to Peter's."

It's a solid plan. Except—Riley's a teenager, so she whines, "*Come on*, the library's on the other side of town."

"That's the thing about cars," I tell her. "They can travel long distances. It's amazing."

She rolls her eyes. "Why do I have to do it?"

"Because you agreed to help drive the kids around when we agreed to buy you a new Camry instead of a used one. That was the deal, Riley," Chelsea answers.

Robert and Rachel McQuaid had a sizable life-insurance policy when they died, so even with six kids to care for, money isn't really an issue for us. The house is paid off, each of the kids has a healthy college fund, and being a founding partner of my own law firm, I do pretty damn well. But—thanks to the advice of my best friend and partner, Brent Mason, who inherited more money than he'll ever be able to spend—we keep that info from the kids. It's important for them to have ambition, to set goals for themselves—I don't want them ever thinking they can waste their lives living off money someone else earned for them.

"Fine." Riley sighs. She looks at her brother. "How long are you going to be at the library?"

Raymond cleans his Harry Potter–like glasses. "Three or four hours."

"Okay—text me when you're ready to be picked up."

Raymond nods.

And just like that, plain old chaos becomes organized chaos.

This is my life now. And it's pretty fucking great.

# CHAPTER TWO

I crouch down and pull out the weeds around the white marble, then brush away the grass clippings clinging to the etched name.

"Hey, Judge!" Ronan's baby-sweet voice chirps. He places a pot of forget-me-nots at the base of the headstone proudly. "We got these for you. They're like the color the sky gets sometimes."

His round eyes look up at me. "Can I go look at the statues?"

I nod, smiling. "Stay where I can see you. And don't run on the graves—it's disrespectful."

"Got it!" He scampers away, toward the large old crypt in the center of the cemetery.

The Judge passed away six months ago, but it feels like he's been gone a lot longer. His last year was rough. Advanced Alzheimer's is a bitch. He stopped speaking, eating, walking. It was almost . . . a relief when he went. Because the real Atticus Faulkner—the man who saved me from prison and from myself—would've never wanted to live the way he was living then.

I used to visit him in the nursing home every week. These days I stop by once a month, to let him know I'm still thinking of him, still grateful for all the things he taught me. And . . . because I just miss him.

"Hey, old man. What's new?"

No, I don't actually expect an answer. Chelsea's Catholic, and so are the kids, but I'm . . . nothing. Our wedding was held at sunset, in the garden outside our reception venue. I would've converted—for her—but Chelsea didn't want to wait as long as we would've had to, to do the deed in a church. I don't know if I even believe in God . . . but the Judge?

I believed in him.

"The scholarship has been running for the last month. We're already getting submissions. Lots of smart kids who've done some stupid shit in their lives."

The Judge didn't have any family, so he left his entire estate to me, with a note: *You'll know what to do with it.* I didn't, at first, and I cursed the son of a bitch for not being more specific. I imagine he got a good laugh over that—he never liked making things too easy for me. But then I got it: The Atticus Faulkner Scholarship. It's open to high school students with difficult backgrounds who can show they're smart and willing to work hard. The scholarship will pay for their education.

"Lots of kids who remind me of me—you'd get a kick out of them."

I hang out at the cemetery a little longer talking to the Judge and watching Ronan running around in circles, like our dog, Cousin It, chasing his tail. Before we head out, I tap the top of the headstone. "See you soon, Judge."

———

Later that afternoon, I'm in the den watching the baseball game. Except for Riley and Raymond, the kids are scattered throughout the house, but it's quiet, which is a rare commodity around here. Chelsea comes in and hands me an iced tea.

"Thanks."

"Sure."

She sits beside me on the couch, facing me, her legs tucked, her pretty feet curled under her. Yes—Chelsea has pretty fucking feet, okay? I never knew feet could be pretty—until I saw hers.

"So . . . that talk I mentioned before? We should probably have that now, while we can."

I take a sip of my drink and nod. "Yeah—I wasn't at all hoping you'd forget about it or anything."

Her face slides into a grin. "Funny."

I look back at her, straight-faced. "I'm a funny guy."

When she doesn't say anything for a few moments, I ask, "What's up?"

Because now I'm actually getting concerned. My stomach tightens as I brace for whatever's worrying her—and before I even know what I'm up against, in my head I'm already planning all the ways I'll take care of it. Because that's what I do—and I'm good at it.

But what she tells me next blows my fucking mind.

"I'm late."

Two words—ten thousand thoughts exploding in my head at once.

I'm a big guy, six-five, 225 pounds of muscle. Guys like me, our voices don't squeak. But at this moment, mine comes damn close.

"Like . . . for an appointment?"

Chelsea's beautiful face is tense and her crystal-blue eyes are iced over with worry. She takes the biggest breath and says, "No."

"Wow."

"Yeah."

"Fucking, wow."

"I know."

I'm guessing couples usually talk about having kids before they get married—but Chelsea and I didn't. Mostly because our plate was already fucking full.

"How . . ." I begin, then stop myself. *Obviously* I know how. "I mean, you're still wearing the patch?"

Chelsea nods. "Yes. But it's not one hundred percent effective and remember a few weeks ago it kept peeling off?"

I'm lucky I remember my own name right now.

My thoughts are still scrambled. Images of a tiny newborn mixed in with the six faces we already have. Ronan was only a few months old when Chelsea and I first met, so I know what's coming. Midnight feedings, teething, crying for no reason at all. And the diapers—fuck—so many diapers. For *years*.

On the other hand, I've heard pregnancy makes a woman's tits huge. My eyes are drawn to Chelsea's already impressive rack. That pro might just outweigh all the cons.

I scrub my hand over my face. "Have you taken a test yet?"

"Not yet."

In the years before Chelsea, I banged lots of women. Hundreds. But I never had a pregnancy scare because I was religious about condoms. There was an STD scare once—because those can happen even with condoms—but this is brand-new territory.

"Okay." I stand up from the couch. "I'll go buy a test."

"I already bought one." She smiles shyly. "I bought three, actually."

"Oh." My brow wrinkles. "Well, let's go take them."

I hold out my hand and pull her up from the couch. As I turn toward the hallway, her hand on my arm stops me.

"Jake . . . where are you on this?" She peers up at me, trying to read my face. "I mean, if I am pregnant . . . are we gonna be okay?"

I'm floored that she even needs to ask.

"Of course we'll be okay." I cup her jaw, holding her gaze. "It's a hell of a shock, sure, but it's not like we don't know what we're doing. Adding one more to the mix . . . will only make it better. Maybe."

When she smiles, it's full and relieved.

I kiss her forehead. "Let's go piss on some sticks."

———

"I couldn't believe it when I didn't get my period. I kept waiting for the cramps to start, I double-checked my calendar, and when the realization finally hit me, I was just like, wow! You know?"

Chelsea's talking a mile a minute. She talked while she took care of the three tests and hasn't stopped to take a breath while we wait to read them. She flutters around the room, like a twittering, gorgeous bird, putting laundry away, shifting things around on the dresser, unable to be still.

"I was thinking I'd like to have the baby down here with us for at least the first year. They're so tiny when they're first born, I don't want to be too far away. I don't know if we'll need to do more construction, to make our room bigger—which will suck—but we have nine months still. There'll be time."

My mouth quirks up as her wheels spin. "Plenty of time." I check my watch. "Speaking of time . . ." I tilt my head toward the bathroom.

Chelsea practically vibrates next to me. "I can't look! You should do it, you look."

"Okay, okay—I'm looking." I chuckle as I walk to the adjoining bathroom to get the tests.

Chelsea's voice follows me. "The kids are going to freak out. Regan and Ronan will be excited—Riley will probably be glad . . ."

I step back into the bedroom slowly, a heavy weight pressing on my stomach.

"Chelsea . . ."

". . . that she's leaving for college in a year. I'll have to talk to my boss at the museum. I wonder—"

"Chelsea." My voice is firmer this time, drawing her smile to my face. "It's negative."

Her smile freezes. "What?"

"They're negative. All of them."

Pink rises in her cheeks and understanding washes over her expression, taking her beautiful smile with it.

"Oh."

She glances at the tests in my hand—and the weight in my stomach is replaced with an empty, sunken feeling.

Chelsea clears her throat and lifts her shoulder. "Well, I guess that's good news then."

"I guess."

But it doesn't seem like good news.

She exhales a big breath and takes the white sticks from me, tossing them in the trash can. Then she moves around the room quickly, rearranging the things on the dresser she just arranged.

"Of course it is. I mean, the last thing we need . . ." She shakes her head. Her back is to me so I can't read her expression. "I must've miscalculated my dates. Stupid. I'll be more careful."

"Chelsea."

She turns around, head down, moving toward the door. "I have laundry to do. Rory needs his uniform tomorrow and—"

Before she gets near the door, I catch her with my arm and pull her in close. She presses her face into my chest and a second later she lets out a deep, choked sob.

Chelsea's not a crier. Or a sulker. She's scrappy, tough in that feminine, enduring, always-making-the-best-of-things kind of way. And I do my damnedest to make sure she doesn't ever have a reason to cry. Because I'm tough, too. Hard. Some would even say callous. Except when it comes to her tears.

They fucking wreck me, every time.

After a minute, she hiccups. "I don't even know why I'm crying."

I stroke the back of her head. "You're crying because you're disappointed. Because, even for just a little while, you thought we were having a baby—and you were happy about it. You *want* to have a baby." My own realization comes just a second before I say the words. "And I do, too."

Her head jerks up, eyes darting over my face. "You do?"

I wipe at her tears with my thumb. "Well, I didn't, up until a few minutes ago. But now . . . yeah . . . the idea of having a kid with your eyes and my bubbly personality . . ."

That gets her laughing because I've been called a lot of things, but *bubbly* will never be on the list.

". . . that would be incredible, Chelsea."

Her brows draw together. "So, what are we saying? Are we going to try and have a baby? Like, actively?"

Some guys would say I'm nuts, to add more time-sucking responsibility, more stress to our family situation. Especially now, when it finally feels like we have a handle on things.

But . . . screw it.

"Yeah, that's what I'm saying. Let's do it." A thought occurs to me and I add, "I mean, if you're sure you want to. This is going to affect you a lot more than it will me. You should consider that."

Chelsea finished her graduate degree in art history just before our wedding. She really likes her job at a small off-shoot of the Smithsonian, but even with a sitter helping out a few days a week, because of the inflexibility of my hours, she's never been able to do more than part-time. A new baby would mean she wouldn't even be able to do that—at least not for a while.

Chelsea wraps her long arms around my neck, reaches up on her tiptoes, and kisses me. It's sweet, and hot at the same time. Needy, but tender, too. When she pulls back, there are still tears in her eyes—but happier ones.

"Let's make a baby, Jake."

# CHAPTER THREE

*September*

Whoever said trying for a baby is hard work is out of their mind. Our sex life was hot before, but once the effectiveness of Chelsea's birth control wore off, it went into overdrive. My wife is creative—she's a sketch artist as well as a curator—but the creative ways she found for us to fuck were nothing short of extraordinary.

On top of our normal, pre-dawn screwing, there was shower sex, lunch-break-on-my-desk at the office sex, on-top-of-the-washing-machine laundry-room sex, putting-away-the-groceries pantry sex. We even defiled the hall closet, which was a tight fit, and yet fantastic at the same time.

Then there was the night we had dinner with Stanton and Sofia, my best friends and partners at the firm, as well as parents to two-year-old Samuel. The four of us knocked back three bottles of wine and when we got home the kids were already fast asleep. So I nailed Chelsea, rough and dirty, over the back of the armchair in the den.

Needless to say, during the course of those weeks, I was a happy son of a bitch.

———

While Chelsea and I were busy trying to make a baby, the rest of the crew was remaining in denial about the arrival of the Best. Month. Ever. For most of my adult life, my calendar revolved around my career as a criminal defense attorney—bail hearings, arraignments, motions, trials. I was indifferent to what month it was, because every month was basically the same.

That all changed when I fell for Chelsea and the McQuaids.

Now, after a long, hot summer with a house full of needy kids, I look forward to September—the same way little ones all over the world look forward to Christmas. Back-to-school displays are up as far as the eye can see, and childhood despair is in the air. September is a good time.

Except . . . for school-supplies shopping.

That blows.

"It's the wrong one," Rosaleen tells me, scrunching her nose up at the folder in my hand.

I check The List—caps intended.

"It's green. How can it be the wrong one?"

She points at the inventory as long as my arm. "It says *lime* green. That's *kelly* green."

Is this school fucking serious?

Annoyed, I jam the folder back into the disaster that is the store shelf and push the cart down the aisle.

"This box has ten crayons, Mommy. The List says I need the eight box," Regan explains to Chelsea, who looks as frustrated as I feel.

"There aren't any eight-crayon boxes, Regan."

The midget shrugs. "Then we have to go to a different store."

There's no way the person who made these lists actually has kids. They should be shot. And at this moment, I would defend the person who shoots them, pro bono. Just saying.

Rory hands me a dictionary. "This only has nineteen thousand words—I need the twenty-one-thousand-word edition." Then he smirks. "Don't want to start the year off on the wrong foot. I need all the right feet I can get."

He's got a point there.

"Jake!" Raymond runs up to me from the end of the aisle. "Can I get this science calculator? It's awesome!"

I glance at the calculator in his hand—it has more buttons than I've ever seen in my life. Only Raymond would get excited about a calculator.

"Sure, kiddo."

"Sweet!"

I push my cart up beside my wife's. "How we doing?"

She sighs. "Twenty items down—only about a hundred left. And that's not counting the epic saga of backpack selection."

I don't remember needing so much shit when I was in school. It was a good day if I had a pencil in my pocket.

Chelsea lifts her purse and gestures to the box under it. A pregnancy test. "I picked this up for us. It says it can show results five days before my period's due, so even though I haven't missed it yet, we can take the test tomorrow morning. Fingers crossed."

Her eyes dance with hope. With excitement. When Sofia was pregnant with Samuel she experienced morning sickness. A lot. So I squeeze Chelsea's shoulder. "Don't worry. The way we've been going at it, you'll be puking your guts out in no time."

She smiles.

Then her lovely face straightens as she remembers something. "Speaking of which, you should talk to Riley today. You didn't forget, did you?"

"No, I didn't forget. Unfortunately."

With sex and pregnancy at the forefront of our thoughts lately, Chelsea thinks it's important that we talk to Riley about safe sex.

And by "we" she means fucking me.

She read somewhere about the positive effect a male relationship has on young girls and she thinks, coming from a guy, the information will have more of an impact.

I get it. It's just going to be the most awkward, uncomfortable conversation I've ever had. And I've had some winners, believe me.

Chelsea runs her hand over my chest. "What's the matter? Big, tough guy like you afraid to talk to a teenage girl?"

I raise an eyebrow. "Afraid? No. Just never thought I'd think of the time I took her to a One Direction concert as the good old days."

Chelsea laughs. Then walks over when Regan calls her to look at puppy-covered notebooks.

"I'm booored," Ronan whines from his seat in my cart.

"We're almost done."

"This sucks." He frowns.

"Don't say 'sucks,'" I tell him in my best "parental" voice. "It's not a nice word."

His devil-cute blue eyes meet mine. "But it *does* suck."

I hold back a grin. Because I have a weakness for the pure honesty kids have at his age—before they learn to weigh their words or shadow their opinions.

I rub his head, messing up his thick blond hair. "Yeah, it does."

———

That afternoon, I bite the bullet and stick my head through Riley's bedroom door—she's lying on her bed, phone in hand.

"Hey."

She plucks an earbud from her ear. "Hey. What's up?"

"Got a second?"

Her long-lashed eyes narrow. "I didn't do it."

Preemptive denial—always suspicious.

"Do what?"

"Whatever you want to talk to me about. It wasn't me."

"Noted." I jerk my head toward the spare bedroom. "Come on."

She gets up and follows, throwing her brown curly hair up into a messy bun. We walk into the yellow-walled spare bedroom a few doors down the hall, and I close the door behind us. Riley sits on the bed with a half-annoyed sigh—like I'm wasting her precious time. As if there weren't a hundred other things I'd rather be doing—like getting a root canal without Novocain.

I cross my arms, look at her, and imagine I'm in court, talking to a witness. Calm, cool, and steady—that's my job. And I'm fucking good at it.

"So . . . you and Peter . . . how's that going?"

Her brow wrinkles. "Uh, fine?"

"Six months is a long time in high school years."

"I guess."

"Is that like a candy anniversary?"

And now she looks even more weirded out. "What are you talking about, Jake?"

"Okay, here's the deal—your aunt and I have noticed that you and Peter seem . . . pretty serious. And . . . we want to make sure you're being *safe*."

The last word hangs heavy in the air. Like one of Cousin It's rancid dog farts.

Riley's face turns a startling shade of fire-engine red. "Oh my God. Is this really happening?"

I pinch the bridge of my nose. "I know, I know, it's fucking awful." Then I open my eyes and tell her the bare honest truth. "But this is important, Riley."

Her eyes hit the floor and she breathes out a quiet, "Okay. But I've already had the sex talk. Like, *years ago*, with my mom. I know about being *safe*."

And there goes the eye roll—it was only a matter of time.

I nod. "Knowing isn't the same as doing. Especially when you're in high school." I open the nightstand drawer and pull out the box of condoms inside it. "So, this is always going to be in here. For you to use. No questions asked. Me or your aunt will replace the box as needed—again, no questions asked, Riley."

Trust me—those are answers I do not want to hear.

"Just to be clear, this isn't us saying we're okay with you having sex. This is us being realistic and wanting you to protect yourself . . . if and when you do."

I put the condoms back in the drawer and lean against the wall, crossing my arms again, as Riley watches me.

"Some guys may try and give you a hard time about using condoms. And as a guy, I'm telling you straight up—*screw them*."

The echo of my own words penetrates.

"I mean, don't! Don't screw them. Ever."

Shit, I'm bad at this.

A quick, awkward chuckle pops out of Riley's mouth.

I rub the scruff on my chin, choosing my words carefully. "I'm not going to be a hypocrite and tell you to wait until you're married . . ."

Though it's very tempting.

"I just want you to remember . . . people can get hurt when they have sex before they're ready. No one's ever been hurt by waiting."

She doesn't say anything and I don't really expect her to— but the contemplative look she's wearing tells me everything she doesn't say. She's hearing me.

"And if anyone ever pressures you or hurts you . . ."

I will tie them to a tree and burn them alive.

". . . if you ever have any questions or you're wondering about something . . . you can talk to us. Me or your aunt— there's nothing you can't tell us. Got it?"

She nods. "Got it."

I dip my chin. "Good."

Riley stands up and we walk to the door. Halfway there, she pauses. "This was really open-minded of you, Jake. And I appreciate you and Aunt Chelsea, you know, swapping gender roles in this situation."

Is that what we did?

"But . . . let's never speak of this conversation again. Sound good?"

All the air rushes out of my lungs. "Jesus Christ, yes. Sounds great."

She gives me a thumbs-up and a smile. It's small and still really embarrassed, but it's a smile.

"Awesome."

———

The next morning, Chelsea and I are right back where we were a few weeks ago, sequestered in our bedroom, counting down the three-minute wait time to read the pee test. Chelsea's more subdued this time, keeping a tight rein on her anticipation.

I sit on the bed, tapping out "Iron Man" on my legs. Anxiety is an uncommon feeling for me—but I'm feeling it now. Because, I want this. For her. Because it'll make her so happy.

And I want it for me, too.

Chelsea pushes a reddish-brown lock behind her ear and stands before me. "It's time. You want me to look?"

I grasp her hips and pull her between my legs, planting a kiss against her sternum.

"I'll do it."

This time around, when I step out of the bathroom, I do it smiling. Big and proud. Actually fucking giddy.

Chelsea doesn't wait for me to say the words. She takes one look at my smile and throws herself straight into my arms.

Because we are well and truly knocked up.

# CHAPTER FOUR

*November*

It's a good thing the sex was so abundant before Chelsea got pregnant. It made the weeks that followed—when the pussy party came to a sad, screeching halt—a lot easier to bear. It was the exhaustion that got to her first. It hit Chelsea like a freight train—not even my mouth between her legs could wake her up.

I didn't take it personally.

Then the puking started. Morning sickness would strike in the afternoon, which—big-picture-wise—was for the best. Because most afternoons she was at the museum, which made keeping the news from the kids a lot easier. Not telling them, until after we were sure everything was up and running, was a decision Chelsea and I made together. One in five pregnancies ends in miscarriage during the first trimester—and if that tragedy happened to us, and the kids knew, we'd be opening a whole can of ugly worms that we didn't want to go anywhere near.

So, for the first few months, we didn't tell anyone. I went with her to the first doctor's appointment. Chelsea cried when she heard the heartbeat, and cried harder during the first ultrasound.

I didn't. Seeing a gray blob on a screen and hearing a whoosh-whoosh sound didn't do anything to me. Didn't make any of it *real*.

I kept that to myself though. Because I'm not a fucking idiot.

———

"So . . . I have big news."

It's a mild, sunny Thursday afternoon and me, Brent, Stanton, and Sofia are having lunch at a bar and grill a couple blocks from our building. Brent leans forward on his elbows as he makes this proclamation, his mischievous baby blues landing on each of us to make sure we're paying attention.

If Peter Pan ever decided to grow up, I imagine he'd look a lot like Brent. He's always had this carefree, spontaneous attitude—and getting married a year and a half ago only brought that out in him more. Because now he's got a partner in crime.

Brent and Kennedy travel a lot on the weekends: white-water rafting, skydiving, *Antiques Roadshow* hunting—they've done it all.

With a smile that won't be stopped, he announces, "Kennedy's pregnant."

Sofia squeals, her long dark hair swaying as she pops up and pulls Brent into a bear hug. Stanton raises his glass, and I reach across the table and slap Brent on the back.

"Congratulations."

"That's awesome, man."

I lean back in my chair with a smirk. "How'd your mother take the news? Did she spontaneously combust?"

Mrs. Mason has been looking forward to a grandchild since Brent hit puberty.

"We haven't told the parents yet. I'm trying to hold off the *Fatal Attraction* stalking for as long as I can. But we're going to have to tell them soon. You know how small Kennedy is— she's already starting to show. If her mother makes a comment about her weight, there's an excellent chance I'll finally tell her to go fuck herself." He takes a sip of his lemonade. "Could make Thanksgiving dinner awkward."

I'm not generally a fan of the word *bitch*, but if there was ever a woman who deserved the label—it's Kennedy's mother, Mitzy Randolph.

"How far along is she?" Sofia asks.

"Three and a half months." And there's a light in Brent's eyes that makes me feel all warm and fuzzy inside.

So warm and fuzzy that even though Chelsea is still a few days shy of the end of her first trimester, I hear myself say, "Well, since we're sharing, I guess I should tell you guys . . . Chelsea's pregnant, too."

There's more squeals from Sofia, and deep, congratulatory chuckles from Stanton.

What I get from Brent is, "Dude, you are *so* screwed."

"Hey," I tell him, "think fast."

Then flip him off with both hands.

He laughs, because if you can't give your friends the finger . . .

"Why is your wife's pregnancy the second coming but Chelsea's screws me over?"

It's not that I really care, but his thought process is usually entertaining.

"Because I don't have six starters already sitting on the bench. I mean, damn, Riley's a senior so she has half a foot out the door—and you're already replacing her." He holds up an open hand. "That being said, if anyone should have dozens and dozens of kids—"

"I think we'll stop at seven," I interrupt.

"—it's you and Chelsea. Congratulations, big guy."

"Thank you."

"When is Chelsea due?" Sofia asks.

"She'll be twelve weeks on Sunday. Due date's in June."

"They might end up sharing a birthday," Brent comments. "Maybe, after they're born, we should set them up. If they get married we'd be related."

"They might be the same sex, genius."

He shrugs. "That's legal now."

"Yeah," I snort, "and there's nothing creepy about an arranged marriage."

Brent holds up his hands. "All I'm saying is if we had listened to our parents, me and Kennedy would've been enjoying relationship bliss a long time ago."

"If either of you needs a babysitter, Presley's always looking to make extra cash when she's up here," Stanton volunteers.

Presley is Stanton's seventeen-year-old daughter with his high school sweetheart, Jenny. She lives most of the year in Mississippi with her mother, stepfather, and two little brothers. Between those two and Samuel, Presley could practically run her own day care at this point.

"Oh, I'm so excited!" Sofia claps her hands. Then to her husband, she says, "It's all happening just like we talked about."

"Talked about?" I ask.

Stanton nods. "Sure. Samuel's out of the baby stage and we're not having any more . . ."

Sofia finishes his sentence—because that's how they roll.

". . . so we've been waiting for you two to get on the ball so we can get our baby fix on . . ."

". . . and then give 'em back," Stanton drawls.

They both nod.

Sofia raises her glass. "To our next generation—may they be smart, talented, and beautiful, just like their parents."

We all drink to that.

Now that I've let the cat out of the bag, it's time Chelsea and I tell the kids.

This should be interesting.

———

The six of them sit around the table . . . looking guilty. *Why?* They remind me of inmates lined up in cell block B, hoping the COs don't find the contraband taped under the toilet. My eyes narrow at each of them, and I wonder what it is I don't know.

"So, we wanted to talk to you tonight because we have some exciting news," Chelsea says, taking my hand on top of the table.

Interrogations will have to wait for another time.

"Are we going on vacation to Aruba?" Riley asks, wide-eyed.

"No," I tell her.

"Florida?" Rory tries.

"It's not a vacation, guys," Chelsea says, much to their disappointment.

"Are we getting another dog?" Regan hopes.

"*No*," Chelsea and I say at exactly the same time.

"Guys—shut up and listen." Raymond always was the helpful one.

Chelsea's eyes dance from child to child, and you can almost feel their anticipation. "Jake and I are having a baby!"

At first, no one speaks. Or moves.

Then Raymond ventures, "Are you, like, adopting?"

"No, honey," Chelsea answers. "I'm pregnant."

Riley's the first to pop up from her chair and hug us. "Congratulations, guys, that's awesome."

"I really wanted another dog," Regan says, gravely disappointed.

Rosaleen leans forward. "Did you guys go to the doctor's to get pregnant? Like Jackie Barbacoa's two moms?"

"No . . ."

She thinks on that. While Rory wants more clarification. "Then how did this happen?"

Chelsea glances at me, then shrugs at the kids. "The old-fashioned way."

Rory's hand goes to his stomach. "I'm gonna puke."

That's when they all start talking at once—except for Raymond, who sits back silently. Dazed.

"What's the old-fashioned way?" Regan asks.

"Wow," Rosaleen comments.

"No, I'm seriously gonna puke."

"What's *old-fashioned* mean?"

Ronan stands on his chair. "I'm not gonna be the littlest anymore? I get to be the boss of someone?"

"That's right," I tell him.

He pumps his fist. "Yes!" Then he starts marching around the table chanting, *"I'm gonna be a boss, I'm gonna be a boss . . ."*

While Rory sprints to the umbrella stand in the corner—gagging.

"Huhhh, huhhh . . ."

"Somebody tell me the old-fashioned way!" Regan yells.

And Rosaleen gets fed up. "It's when the man and woman fall in love and the man puts his penis in the woman's vagina and nine months later a baby comes out of it."

Regan looks at me like I'm a monster.

"You put your *penis* in Mommy's *vagina*?"

Christ, this went downhill quick.

"Why would you *do* that?"

*". . . I'm gonna be a boss . . ."*

"We'll talk about that when you're older."

*"Huhhh, huhhh . . ."*

"And now a baby's gonna crawl out of you?!"

"Not exactly."

"You're so immature, Regan."

"Shut up, Rosaleen."

*"Huhh . . ."*

Ronan puts the icing on the cake. "How big *is* your vagina, Mommy?"

And I try to be helpful.

"It's not that big."

As soon as the words are out of my mouth, Chelsea's head whips to me. And we both crack the fuck up.

She covers her eyes with one hand, waving at the kids. "You're crazy. You guys are all crazy."

But they're not even listening to her.

As the chaos continues to erupt, I put my arm around Chelsea's shoulders and pull her against me, kissing her temple. "I think that went well."

# CHAPTER FIVE

*December*

By the first week in December, Chelsea's sporting a small, firm baby bump. Her morning sickness has abated and she says she feels better than ever. Well enough to accept the extra work her boss has been sending her way at the museum—she's been going in early and staying late whenever she can.

She's also slightly obsessed over what she eats—determined to stay away from anything processed or non-organic, but with some coaxing, she gives in to her craving for Double Stuf Oreos dunked in a glass of whole milk.

Around the same time, I get a big case—that's getting national media coverage. It's a string of bank robberies, and despite my client's alibi, the prosecutor has rock-solid DNA evidence on a ski mask that was worn during the crimes. It's the kind of case I craved back in the day—a challenge. A gauntlet with the promise of legal glory at the finish line. And I'd be lying if I said I didn't enjoy digging into it, burying myself in motions and maneuvers to outsmart my opponent. It's easy to do during the day, at the office, but when night creeps in and the sky turns black outside my window, the case feels more like a nuisance.

Because I just want to go home. Pet my dog, see my kids, and screw my wife.

One night, about a week before Christmas, I pack it in fairly early—about seven thirty. When I walk through the front door, Cousin It attacks my shoes, and the house smells of the fire burning in the den fireplace and warm gingerbread cookies. There's loud laughs and shouting coming from the dining room, so I put my briefcase down and head in. The kids are all there around the table, and so are Stanton, Sofia, Presley, Samuel, Brent, and Kennedy.

There's bowls of white icing, and colorful candies, white-and-red-striped peppermint sparkles, scattered all over the table. And about two dozen rectangular pieces of brown cookie.

"Honey, you're home!" Brent greets me, then he sucks one of Kennedy's icing-covered fingers into his mouth.

Regan, Ronan, and Rosaleen attack me at once, talking at the same time, showing me what they're doing. I can only make out every other word. Then Chelsea walks in, wearing a red-and-green apron and carrying a tray of more brown cookie rectangles.

"Hey!" she says with excitement, putting the tray down and reaching up to peck my lips.

"What's going on?" I ask.

She glances around the table. "I went overboard with the gingerbread. So instead of building a house, we're building a town."

Stanton passes me a cold beer from the ice bucket on the end of the table. "Welcome to the party."

Two-year-old Samuel squeals as Sofia tickles him, murmuring something in Portuguese. Then he pops a candy in his mother's mouth.

"Check it out, Jake." Rory motions to the half-constructed building in front of him. "Me and Brent are making the law firm. Becker, Mason, Santos, Shaw and *McQuaid*—has a pretty nice ring to it, don't you think?"

Kennedy answers before I can. "You should think about being a prosecutor, Rory. We have a great office building."

Brent scoffs. "Don't listen to her—she lies. Her office is shit small."

Kennedy plops a glob of icing on Brent's nose.

But he's not bothered at all. "Now you have to lick that off, Wife."

She adds a red M&M to the center of the icing. Taking the cue, Regan screeches, "Food fight!"

"Noooo!" Chelsea laughs. "No food fighting."

Brent shakes his head at his wife. "You're such a bad example."

Kennedy just sticks her tongue out at him.

"Presley and I are making the capitol building," Raymond tells me from the other end of the table. "Together."

Then, behind the seventeen-year-old's back, he gives me a thumbs-up and wiggles his eyebrows. That crush is still going strong.

Chelsea takes my hand. "Come on, grab a chair. What should we make?"

Sometimes I look around and wonder, how the hell did I get here? How is this my life? It all changed so fast. But then

I stop wondering. Because how this life became mine doesn't really fucking matter. I'm just crazy-happy that it is.

"Let's make our house," I tell Chelsea.

Her eyes flare. "Good one. Let's do it."

———

On Christmas morning the kids converge on our bedroom at 4 a.m.—it's the one day they're allowed to come in without knocking. When wrapping paper covers every inch of the floor, and the dog and the kids are busy figuring out their new toys, I set Chelsea up with a cup of tea on the couch, while Rosaleen and I start making enough strawberry-and-blueberry pancakes to feed an army.

Rosaleen whisks a huge bowl of batter while I slice the strawberries.

And out of nowhere, she asks, "Do you think you'll like the baby more than us?"

The knife in my hand freezes. "What?"

She shrugs, blond curls jiggling. "We'll understand if you do."

It takes me a second to come up with an adequate response.

"You know how in school they tell you, 'there are no stupid questions'?"

"Yeah?"

"They're lying to you."

She snorts but doesn't meet my eyes, focusing hard on her bowl.

"Why would you ask me that?"

"Well . . . the baby will be yours. Yours and Aunt Chelsea's."

I put the knife on the counter, wipe my hands, and crouch down to her eye level. When those sweet blue eyes are on me, I give her the firm, irrefutable truth.

"*You* are mine. Mine and Aunt Chelsea's. Never doubt that."

The words sink in . . . and then, slowly, she smiles. And her grin is brighter than all the Christmas lights on this street put together.

"Okay."

I nod and stand up. "Now let's get these pancakes made before your brothers start eating the tree."

# CHAPTER SIX

*January*

After a relatively quiet New Year's, the kids head back to school. Being home with them over the break, I noticed Raymond was really quiet. Too quiet.

So, one day, when Chelsea's boss calls her in early to the museum, and I'm in charge of getting them on the bus, I hold Rory back at the front door.

"What's up with him?"

Rory follows my gaze toward his twin brother's back. Then he shrugs. "Raymond worries."

This isn't news to me. Like many intelligent children, Raymond has anxieties: global warming, droughts, nuclear war—if there's a possibility of worldwide catastrophe, Raymond's shitting a brick about it.

"What's he worried about these days? Specifically."

Rory's gaze turns cautious, reminding me of a witness on the stand. "I can't tell you. It's a brother-code kind of thing. But . . . Raymond doesn't have a password on his laptop. If I was a smart guy—that's where I'd look to find out what's going on."

Then he heads down the driveway. "Later, Jake."

"Yeah, have a good day, kid."

I wait in the front until they all get on the bus. Then I head straight to Rory and Raymond's room. They're twins, but from the looks of their room, you wouldn't think they were even related. The top bunk—Raymond's—is neatly made with hospital corners; the bottom is a ball of blankets, crushed pillows, and mangled sheets. One desk is a disaster area covered in papers, video-game controllers, empty soda cans. The other desk is just-dusted shiny and clean—save for the closed silver MacBook Pro laptop sitting dead center.

I'm sure some parents would feel guilty about invading their kid's private space, but I'm not one of them. Kids can have privacy when they move out.

I fire up the laptop and open Raymond's recent search history. What I read makes my stomach hit the floor.

"Shit."

———

That afternoon, I come home early so I can talk to Raymond before he slides any deeper into his black hole of anxiety. Chelsea is pleasantly surprised. I get a nice, wet kiss when I walk into the kitchen—with tongue. Her hands comb over my shoulders, and her eyes are shiny and teasing. "Wow, I almost don't recognize you in the daylight."

I place my palm on her protruding belly and rub it hello. "I'm the guy who knocked you up—in case you weren't sure."

She smiles against my lips when I pull her in for another kiss.

Ronan abandons his crayons on the kitchen table and runs into the living room, squealing, "Regan, give me my turn on the Wii or I'm gonna knock you up!"

Why do kids only hear the things you don't want them to? Every fucking time.

Chelsea hides her face against my chest. "That phrase is going to go over well in kindergarten tomorrow."

My hand glides down her back. "I'll talk to him. But first I want to talk to Raymond—where is he?"

"He's in the back, shooting hoops. Anything I should know about?"

Worries are contagious—they spread from one person to another like a virus. That's the last thing she needs right now.

"No—it's a guy thing."

She pauses, reading my face—then shrugs. "Okay. Have fun with that."

I head out the back French doors and walk down the path to join Raymond on the blacktop, where he dribbles a basketball.

"Hey."

"Hey." I hold up my hands and he passes me the ball. I bounce it twice, then smoothly shoot it through the hoop.

"What's up?" I ask him as he retrieves the ball.

He shoots, misses. "Nothing."

Raymond shoots again, and I catch the ball after it falls through the net. "You know you can talk to me, right?"

"Yeah, I know," he answers automatically.

"About anything. Nothing you say would ever change what I think of you. Understand?"

During my years as a pissed-off, defensive little punk, the Judge probably said those same words to me a dozen times. My mother—probably a hundred. But I never got it.

Now I do.

Because there really is nothing any of these kids could ever say or do—no outrage too great, no mistake too stupid—that would make me stop loving them with every fiber of my being.

Raymond answers cautiously, his blue eyes squinting behind his round, black-wire frames. "You're being really weird, Jake."

"I saw the search history on your computer, Raymond."

I pass the ball to him quickly. He catches it with two hands and stares at me.

"You did?"

"Yeah." I lift my chin toward the bench. "Sit down."

Raymond sits down on the bench, the ball in his lap, watching me as I take up the rest of the bench beside him. "You looked on my computer?"

I nod. "Feel free to be indignant about that later, but right now, I want to talk about the things you're looking up—why you're so anxious, not sleeping." I lean over, bracing my elbows on my spread knees. "What's going on with you, buddy?"

His throat ripples as he swallows. Then he looks away and his voice is hushed, like he's afraid to say the words too loudly. "Did you know, the number one cause of death for pregnant women is murder?"

I do know that. Just one of the fun fucking facts criminal defense attorneys get to know. A woman is never more vulnerable—in every conceivable way—than when she's carrying a child.

Raymond doesn't wait for me to answer. "But one thousand ninety-five women died last year—in childbirth. Healthy women. And that's not counting the thousands who died from pregnancy-related complications."

"Raymond—"

"Diabetes, hypertension, blood clots—all kinds of things can go wrong."

"Raymond—"

"Placenta abruption, infection, hemorrhaging—a human being can bleed out in under one hundred and twenty seconds. Sometimes—"

"Raymond, *stop*." My voice snaps the air, like the crack of a whip.

He blinks at me, his pale lips going still. I put my hand on his shoulder and squeeze. "None of those things are going to happen to your aunt."

"You don't know that."

"I'm not going to *let* them happen."

He shakes his head slowly. "You can't protect her from it."

"Yes, I fucking can."

Raymond shoots to his feet. "No, you can't! If you want to lie to the other kids so they're not scared, go ahead—but don't lie to me. I know better. And so do you."

He breathes hard, looking at me like he can read my thoughts, see my deepest fears. I scrub my hand down my face, glance to the spot beside me, and say, "Sit."

After he's settled back on the bench, I force confidence into my voice. Because optimism isn't one of my better traits. But I have to say something.

"There are dangers in pregnancy—yes—but obsessing over statistics and every freak possibility isn't going to help anything. You have to think positively."

He stares down at the blacktop between his feet, and his voice falls even softer. Monotone.

"The night my parents got into the accident, we were with a babysitter. She was in college, I think—one of my dad's interns. She didn't tell us they were . . . gone. Only that they'd been in a car accident, that Aunt Chelsea was on her way. She said we should think good thoughts, and pray." He looks up at me with shiny eyes, drowning with remembered grief. "So I did. I prayed really hard, Jake." His voice breaks, choking on the words. "It didn't help."

Raymond turns away as his face crumples. Because he's thirteen years old—and boys aren't supposed to cry. But I wrap my arm around him, pull him tight against me.

Because as far as I'm concerned, he can cry all he fucking wants.

His shoulders shudder and his face presses against my shirt. I rest my lips on his dark hair—which smells like grass and still-childish sweat. And my heart breaks for him, because there's nothing I can say. No words to make this better. It's just something he has to feel. Go through.

All I can do is hold on to him.

When the worst of it seems to pass, when his shaking turns to sniffling, I crouch down in front of him, my hands on his bony knees. "Raymond, sometimes, in life, brutal, unfair things happen to us. You don't need me to tell you that. But there's a lot of good, too. Unexpected, beautiful good. And if you spend all your time worrying about the bad stuff, you might miss out on enjoying all the amazing things. I don't want that for you—your parents wouldn't want that for you, either."

He wipes his nose with the back of his hand. "Are you scared? For Aunt Chelsea?"

I tilt my head. "Well, I am now. Thanks for that."

He snorts—a wet, clogged sound—because he knows I'm teasing.

But, then, I realize I'm not.

"Yeah. Sometimes I get scared."

"What do you do when that happens?"

I blow out a breath. "I focus on the things I can change, on the things I can do to make a difference. I mean, you have to know that your aunt is young and she has the best doctors—so the odds that this will happen without a single problem are really good."

He nods. "Yeah, I know that."

I squeeze his leg. "Then here's what we're going to do—you and me together. We'll take care of her, make sure she rests and eats right, and we'll think about how nuts and awesome it's going to be to have a baby in the house again."

That prompts a small smile.

"And when you get scared, when those dark worries creep up on you, you don't look at your computer in the middle of the night. You bring those worries to me, okay? Because you're not alone, Raymond. We'll talk about it and figure things out together. Can you do that for me?"

Raymond takes his glasses off, dries them on his T-shirt, then slides them back on.

"Yeah, Jake, I can do that."

"Thanks, buddy."

I give his head another hug as I stand—smacking him on the back.

"Let's head inside for dinner."

Raymond peers out into the backyard. "I'm gonna stay out here for a few minutes if that's okay?"

"Sure. Totally okay."

I walk back toward the house but only make it a few steps before Raymond calls my name. When I turn around, he says, "You know, Jake, my dad was a really great dad."

I smile. "I know. I can tell by how you guys are turning out."

Raymond thinks for a moment, choosing his words. "You're pretty great at the dad stuff, too."

Kids are incredible—their insight, their capacity to adapt and accept, grow and love. They're powerful, too. We'd all be in some seriously deep shit if they ever realized just how much power they have over us. Because the warm, tingling, insanely proud, totally devoted feeling that spreads through me—it's indescribable. And Raymond did that. He gave me that.

I clear my throat. "Thanks, Raymond. That . . . means a lot."

He nods. And then goes back to playing basketball.

And I head into the house to kiss my wife again, and help take care of the other minions.

———

Later that night, after homework is done, the dishes are clean, and the kids are all tucked in their beds, I sit alone at the kitchen table with a bottle of scotch and a half-empty glass in front of me. Chelsea walks in, her hair pinned up from her bath, dressed in cotton, pastel-pink pajamas. Her steps slow when she sees me. And I feel her eyes drift to the bottle, then back to me.

She knows me, inside and out—knows I'm not a drinker. Unless there's a reason. So she pulls out a chair and quietly sits down. The crystal-blue eyes that own my dreams, hold me in their grasp.

"What's going on, Jake?"

I sip the scotch, then watch the amber liquid bob when I set the glass back down on the table. My voice comes out hushed but certain. "I would pick you."

"What do you mean?"

Finally, I look up at her, and I know my face is clouded with guilt. "In that scenario that always plays out on TV shows, when the doctors tell the father he has to choose between the life of the baby or the life of the mother . . . I would pick you."

Her head tilts to the side and her voice is so soft. "I would want you to pick the baby."

"I know. I know that." I stare into her eyes. "But I would still pick you."

Is that as fucked-up as it feels? I raise the glass to my lips, draining it empty, trying to wash the feeling away.

And my whispered words slice the stillness of the moment. "All of this only works if you're here. It begins with you, it ends . . ."

I'm not good with flowery, romantic kinds of words. But she makes me wish I was.

Because she's more than my wife—more than the owner of the pussy that has me so very whipped. She's my love, my home, the solace to my soul, the keeper of my heart, the center of my entire fucking world. The only reason I really believe in my own goodness is because I see it reflected in her eyes.

"Without you, I don't know how . . . I don't know what I'd do."

A sad smile haunts Chelsea's rosy lips as she rises and plants herself on my lap. My arms automatically wrap around her.

"I know what you would do." Her fingers comb through my hair soothingly, rubbing at the base of my neck. "You would hold all the kids at once, because your arms are big enough to do that. And you'd let them all sleep in the bed with you, so you could be right there if they needed you. Then, after a few days, you'd lead them through it—get them back on schedule. Back to the routine. You'd still be broken inside, but you would tape yourself together because you'd know that's what they needed." Her warm lips press against my jaw and her breath tickles my neck. "Life would go on. And after some time, you'd meet someone. A kind woman. Smart. Maybe a lawyer who always wanted kids but never found the time."

"Jesus fucking Christ, Chelsea," I curse—because I don't want to hear this.

"She would fall in love with you so easily. And with them. And it would all be okay. It would be a good life—a different life, but still good."

My eyes burn behind my eyelids, because I don't want any part of that fucking life. She's right, in a way—I would go on—just like I'd want her to. You don't have a whole lot of choice when you have kids—when you love them like you're supposed to. You suck it up. Move heaven and hell to make sure they're all right.

But it'd be a waking nightmare for me—every horrible second without her.

My hands press her closer. Melancholy fingers scrape her back, her thigh. "Don't ever leave me. Promise me you'll be with me always. I know it's not a promise you can make . . . but do it anyway."

Chelsea punctuates each word with a gentle kiss—to my forehead, my nose, my jaw, my cheeks, my closed eyelids. "Never. I'll never leave you, Jake Becker. Ever. Ever. Ever. Ever. Ever. Ever. Ever . . . never."

When her mouth settles on mine it's like lighting a match. Sparking a needy, frantic fire. Because I have to feel her—alive and vibrant—beneath me, surrounding me.

I should take her to our room, but I don't. I should slow down, but I can't.

All I can do is set her on the table and strip the fabric from her body with trembling hands. Kiss her like there's never been a tomorrow, lick her skin and swallow her moans.

I grip the back of my shirt, pulling it off, and my pants follow. My fingers rub and delve between her legs, feeling sleek, slippery wetness, and then I'm pushing inside her. That first thrust—the slide of her smooth, tight walls against my hot, hard cock. *Fucking unreal.* Like it's always been with her. Like it always will be. Her body welcomes me, then clamps down like it can't bear for me to leave. And just like every time before, the thought flits through my mind, that nothing will ever feel better than this—it's as good as it can ever possibly be.

And just like every time before, I'm proven so fucking wrong.

My strokes are steady and long, more demanding, harsher than they should be. I cradle Chelsea's head in my hands, my fingers pulling her hair free so it cascades down her flawless back. Her feet lock around my waist, pulling me closer, and our chests meld together. The solid swell of her stomach, where our child sleeps, presses against my lower abdomen. Chelsea tilts her head back, holding on to my gaze for as long as she can— until it's too much. And the feverish, rising, fucking sublime pleasure forces her lids to close and her lips to part.

I curl over her, my hand tightening in her hair, my hips driving faster.

"Jake . . . Jake . . ." She comes hard, her muscles contracting, the gasp of my name on her perfect lips.

Then Chelsea goes slack, cradled safely against my chest. I slip my hands under her ass, lifting her off the table—plunging inside her again and again with wild, barely controlled abandon. Her hands cling to my shoulders. Trusting me, taking me, giving me everything I could ever need.

My hips circle, drag, and then with a final thrust and ragged groan, I come so deep inside her.

For several long moments, my lips rest against the top of her head, smelling the sweet clean of her hair, while her hands trace up and down my spine. The storm of guilt and apprehension churning in my gut quiets. Because that's the power she has, this lithe wisp of a woman—her voice calms me, and her touch gives me peace.

Chelsea's face lifts to mine, wearing a drowsy but satiated grin. "Better?"

I play with her hair. "Yeah. Better."

"Good. Now I need another bath. You got me all dirty."

My lips smile easily now. "I like you dirty."

She nips at my shoulder. "Feel like joining me?"

I let her go just long enough to grab our clothes from the floor. Then she's back in my arms and I'm guiding us down the hall. "Absolutely."

# CHAPTER SEVEN

*February*

Chelsea came home late from work again last night—after nine. Not that I mind doing my part with the kids—but being five months pregnant she should be taking it easier. So early the next morning, I head over to the museum to chat with her moron of a boss. I know Chelsea won't be in until the afternoon.

I've only met the guy once, but I'm giving him the benefit of the doubt that he's just a moron—not a total dickwad—who doesn't realize the extra projects, the staying later to "help out" shit needs to stop. Chelsea loves this job, so I'll be nice about it.

At least—nice is the plan.

That plan goes up in smoke when I stand outside Gavin Debralty's open office door, out of sight, but within earshot of the two men inside.

"Chelsea getting knocked up sucks for you, Gavin—I know how badly you wanted to get up in there."

I hear a slimy-sounding snort in reply, and then, "Oh, I'm still getting up in there—count on it. Just need to speed things up before she gets too fat." They chuckle, and my blood turns to ice. "Though I guess it won't make a difference if she's a hundred pounds or three hundred—those lips will feel just as good around my cock."

Some people talk about their anger like an explosion—boiling lava, blistering fury. But I don't work that way. My rage is cold. Detached, callous, brutally unyielding.

You know the difference between a scalding and frostbite?

A burn takes off skin. Frostbite will take your whole fucking limb off.

I step into the doorway, my fists clenched at my sides like two hammers. The piece of shit Gavin was talking with—a coworker of Chelsea's I met at the Christmas party—pales to a sickly white when he spots me.

"Crap."

Gavin turns around and meets my gaze. For a second he looks surprised, maybe even afraid, then his expression slides slack with indifference. The kind of countenance that says he thinks he can do anything, say anything, and tough tits to anyone who doesn't like it.

He should enjoy that feeling. Won't last long.

His companion mumbles an excuse and smartly scurries around me out the door. Gavin turns to face me as I step into the room, rolling his blond head on his neck, lifting his average-size shoulders, like he's loosening up for a fight.

Such a dumb fuck.

Too stupid to realize he'll never have the chance to take a swing.

"Listen," he starts, "sorry you had to hear that, but—bro to bro—I gotta tell you, your little wifey has been on my jock since day one. The way she—"

His words cut off—along with his air—when my hand lashes out and wraps around his windpipe. I press him back against the nearest wall. Squeezing.

"Another word," I tell him softly, "and I'll rip your throat out."

Before the Judge took me under his wing, I had a nasty temper. With his help, I learned to lock it down. But that's the thing about rage—it never really goes away; it just sleeps. Mine's wide awake at the moment, pounding against the bars of its cold cage, begging to be set loose.

Just for a few minutes. That's all it needs.

Gavin's face starts to redden and his fingers claw pathetically at my hand as I lean in close and tell him, "I'm going to ask you some questions—you'll nod or shake your head to respond. If you lie, I'll know, and I'll hurt you."

His struggle lessens and I take that to mean he understands.

"Have you ever touched Chelsea?"

He shakes his head frantically.

"Have you ever scared her?"

Another shake in the negative.

"Have you ever made her feel uncomfortable?"

There's an infinitesimal pause—then he gives me another shake of his head. I release his throat, but before he can draw a breath, my fist drives up deep into his diaphragm. Because that last answer was a fucking lie.

He doubles over, gagging on air and retching bile. I yank him back up, eye to eye. "Here's what's going to happen, Gavin. Chelsea's not coming back here—she quits—consider this her resignation. From now on, you don't think about her, you sure as shit don't talk about her. If you glimpse her on the street, you run the other way and make damn certain she doesn't see you. You're going to write her a reference letter, so she can get another job that doesn't include a sniveling scumbag like yourself. And that reference better be radiant, Gavin—every word of glowing praise we both know she's earned. Put it in an envelope, tape it to the outside of your office door, and don't be here when she picks it up."

He nods, still wheezing.

My voice is low, deadly. "You fuck with my wife, you fuck with me. And in case you haven't realized it yet, I'll spell it out for you: you do *not* want to fuck with *me*."

The rage inside, the one with my father's voice, clamors for at least one broken bone—his arm, his jaw, his fucking spine.

But the image of six sweet, smiling faces who need me, holds me back, gives me the strength to walk out the door, and leave Gavin Debralty bruised but not broken.

———

I use the walk from the museum to the law firm to pull my shit together. By the time I walk into the conference room for our weekly meeting, I assume I look normal again.

And . . . I'd be wrong about that.

Stanton, Sofia, and Brent stare at me with wide eyes as I sit down. For several long seconds, no one speaks. Then Stanton ventures, "You all right, man?"

I glare at the file on the table in front of me. "Why wouldn't I be?"

Sofia tucks her long dark hair behind one ear. "Don't take this the wrong way, but you look kind of . . . murderous, Jake."

"That makes sense." I grind my jaw. "Almost just killed a guy. I didn't—but I could have."

Brent's eyebrows lift high. "Well, there's something you don't hear every day—even in this business."

Stanton leans forward. "Maybe you should elaborate . . . just in case."

That's probably a good idea.

After I tell them the whole story, Brent and Stanton are firmly on my side. They get it.

Sofia? Not so much.

"Wait a second. You quit her job for her? And you think Chelsea is going to be okay with that?"

In retrospect—probably not. And yet, I can't make myself give even a single fuck.

Because I'm pissed that she didn't tell me the cocksucker she works for was making her uncomfortable. That she's likely been dealing with his looks and suggestions—and *Christ* that better be all she's been dealing with—on her own.

"What other choice did he have, Soph?" Stanton asks. "I sure as shit wouldn't want you working for a dickhead like that."

Sofia's eyes narrow—because she is woman, and she's never been shy with the roaring.

"Why does Chelsea have to leave a job she loves and the *dickhead* gets to stay?"

Brent adds his two cents. "She's got a point, Jake. I learned the hard way not to mess with my girl's career—remember?

On the other hand, Chelsea will be going on maternity leave soon."

"And she had the option of going back after the baby's born," Sofia counters. "But now that option is gone."

On that note, my phone alarm chirps. Because my ass needs to be in court in twenty minutes.

On the way over, Sofia's comments start to sink in and I decide to at least give Chelsea a heads-up about what I've done. I try to call her, but she doesn't pick up. If Gavin has half a brain cell, he'll do what I told him . . . and Chelsea and I will be discussing the aftermath face-to-face.

———

Court adjourns early, so I make it home by four. Early enough to send home the babysitter, who's usually there when the kids get off the bus. Chelsea typically works until six on Wednesdays, but I'd be lying if I said I wasn't surprised that she's not home earlier today.

There's a din of chatter around the dining room table as the kids bustle around, simultaneously unpacking backpacks, talking about homework, asking to go to friends' houses, wondering what's for dinner, and seeking permission to have a snack. I sit in a chair at the end of the table, legs stretched out, arms folded—eyes glued to the doorway.

Until I hear the front door slam open with a meaningful bang.

And my gorgeous, pregnant wife appears, pinning me down with the blue fucking fire in her eyes.

She breathes out hard through her nose "We need to talk. Outside. Now."

The kids all freeze midmotion. In any other case, it'd be funny—the way their attention is instantly captured.

"We sure do," is my simple reply.

Raymond starts to whistle the Darth Vader theme from *Star Wars*.

As I stand and follow Chelsea toward the kitchen, Rosaleen sings, "Someone's in trouble."

"And for once, it's not me," Rory points out. "Take note, people."

———

Through the kitchen and out the back door onto the patio we go. As soon as the door is shut, Chelsea whips around, waving an opened envelope at me.

"What the hell is this? And why did Gavin inform me— through his closed office door, I might add—that you'd given him my resignation?"

I cross my arms. "I'm more interested in hearing about the sexual harassment you've been silently suffering for God knows how long and why the hell you didn't clue me in on it."

Now she crosses her arms and cocks a hip. "I like my job, Jake—it wasn't that bad—and I knew you'd make a big deal about it."

I keep a tight rein on my voice—and my temper—though I gotta say, it's a battle.

"Hearing that cocksucker tell your coworker how he couldn't wait for you to blow him sounded like a pretty fucking big deal to me. Guess I'm funny like that."

She blinks up at me. "He said that?"

My nod is quick and sharp. "And his choice of words wasn't nearly as nice." I point my finger. "You should've told me you were dealing with that."

"I was handling it!"

Those four words push me right to the edge. "You obviously weren't handling it, since the scumbag was still spewing shit about you. That won't be a problem anymore."

Her jaw is clenched and her chin is high—and if I wasn't genuinely fucking furious, I'd be really turned on right now.

"I'm not quitting my job, Jake."

"You already have."

"I'm *not* quitting my job, Jake."

My voice goes soft, dropping to a lethal whisper. "Let me make this crystal clear. If that fucker gets within twenty feet of you ever again, I will put him in the ground. You're not going back there. Period."

Chelsea's arms flail out to her sides and she yells, "Who *are* you?"

"I'm your husband."

"Really? I don't remember exchanging rings with a fucking caveman!"

I lean down over her, almost nose to nose. "Then you weren't paying close enough attention."

She glares up at me for a few seconds; then she closes her eyes and breathes deep, stepping back. When she focuses on me again, the fury has faded—replaced with something more dangerous. Resentment.

"I can't talk to you when you're like this."

"I'm completely calm. You're the one pitching a fit. And apparently you can't fucking talk to me *at all*."

It seems I've got some resentment issues of my own. Brent would say this is healthy—getting it all out in the open. That theory can go suck a dick.

Chelsea's hand goes to her stomach—to the bump—rubbing circles. She takes another deep, cleansing breath. "The kids have homework, we have to start dinner, Rosaleen's piano teacher will be here any minute. We'll finish this later."

She moves around me to the door but stops when I call her name.

"Chelsea. It's already finished."

She hisses at me through clenched teeth, "God, you are such an asshole sometimes!"

"Whatever."

After that, we do our best to ignore each other the whole fucking night.

———

Dinner? Done.

Dishes? Clean.

Kids? Asleep. Or at least, pretending to be, which works for me.

Chelsea and I share the bathroom sink space, brushing our teeth, our arms moving in matching, violent jerks, both of us avoiding the mirror and instead glaring at the faucet like it insulted our mother.

I finish first, walk into the bedroom, strip down to boxer briefs, and slide between the cold sheets. A minute later the bathroom light goes out, and I watch, through the moonlit, shadowed room, as Chelsea walks around to the other side of the bed. She climbs in—staying as far away from me as she possibly can without actually falling off the mattress.

I stare at the ceiling, one arm slung above my head, listening to the sound of her tense, harsh breaths. And God, I know it makes me sound like a pussy—but I want to hold her. As frustrated as I am with her ridiculous stubbornness, as infuriated as I feel about the entire fucking debacle . . . I love her.

It's a constant, living, needy thing inside me. My arms twitch with the urge to pull her close, to feel her, warm and supple against me.

My voice comes out in a gentle, jagged whisper.

"Chelsea . . ."

Slowly, she turns on her side, facing me. We watch each other in the darkness for a few seconds, then she insists softly, "Our discussion is not over."

"Okay."

"And I'm going to be really mad at you again in the morning."

My hand finds her jaw, stroking, before moving through her hair. "I can live with that."

She gives me a tiny nod, and then—she moves in close, resting her head on my chest. I wrap my arm around her, holding tight. And there's a small comfort in the idea she needs this every bit as much as me.

"I love you, Chelsea."

Her sigh is long but not ungrateful.

"I know. I love you, too."

There's a weighted pause, and then she adds, "Even when you're being an asshole."

Yep. I can totally live with that.

———

The next morning, our midnight truce is most definitely off. Our mornings are busy—crazy—and that's never truer than on a school day. I get the kids up. They're dressed and almost fed by the time Chelsea walks into the dining room.

Wearing a pretty, dark-green sheath dress and matching blazer. Dressed for work.

From the chair at the table, my eyes rake over her.

"Nice outfit."

She smiles tightly. Determinedly. "Thanks. It's new. Maternity clothes have come a long way since Rachel was pregnant."

I cock a questioning brow. "Do you have a job interview lined up already?"

And her nostrils flair. "No. I have a job. I'm dressed to go to it."

At some point during the night, I decided I wasn't going to fight with her anymore. She's fucking pregnant—only an honest-to-goodness coldhearted prick would upset his pregnant wife, and I've put a lot of effort through the years into not being that.

So I nod. Take out my cell phone and dial Brent's number. And as I speak to him, my gaze doesn't waver from my wife's stubborn face.

"Hey. Listen—I'm supposed to be in court today at ten and I'm not gonna make it. Can you stand in for me? Request a continuance?"

Chelsea flinches at the question.

After Brent responds in my ear, I tell him, "Yeah, exactly. Thanks—I owe you."

I jab at the disconnect button and slide the phone into my pocket.

And all eyes—mine and the kids'—are on Chelsea.

"What'd you do that for?"

I open my palms, gesturing like the answer is obvious. "We're going to work at the museum. I'm pretty frigging talented but even I can't be in two places at once."

Her eyes narrow. "You're coming to work with me?"

I smirk viciously. "There's no place else I'd rather be."

"That's your plan? You're going to follow me around. Forever?"

I lean forward, elbows on my knees. "I'll do what I need to do, sweetheart, for however long I need to do it."

Her face pinches and she looks away from me. Then she yanks her own phone out of her blazer pocket and a few seconds later speaks into it—leaving a voice mail.

"Gavin, it's Chelsea. It seems that what you told me yesterday is accurate. I'm resigning. I . . . good-bye." She pins me to the chair with a scowl. "There, you win. Happy, Jake?"

"This isn't about winning."

"You sure? Because that's how it feels."

She turns away, heading into the kitchen, but not before I see the tears welling in those crystal-blue eyes.

And—fuck—if that doesn't make me feel like the smallest dick that's ever existed.

Just when I think I can't feel any lower, Regan manages to help me out.

"Are you and Mommy getting divorced?"

Rory raises his hand. "I call Jake."

Riley swats his hand and tells him to shut up.

I touch Regan's little head. "No, we're not getting divorced."

"That's what Abigail Stillwater's parents said. Right before they got divorced. Then on Visiting Day Mr. Stillwater called Mrs. Stillwater's friend an underage boy toy and Mrs. Stillwater said Mr. Stillwater was a deadbeat bastard who didn't own her. They had to be escorted from the building."

*Jesus Christ.*

Ronan steps up next to his sister. "Are you sure you're not gonna get divorced?" He wags his finger. "Tell the truth."

"Yes, I'm sure." I rub my hand over my face. "Look, guys . . . sometimes adults disagree. Just like you two—you fight all the time, but you still love each other."

They glance at each other, confused—and slightly disgusted.

"We do?"

*Fuck me.*

"Okay, bad example. I promise Mommy and I are not getting divorced." I gesture to their backpacks and coats. "Now get ready—the bus will be here soon. Rosaleen, help Ronan with his shoes."

Rosaleen purses her lips, quieter than I've ever seen her. "Okay."

With a big breath I walk into the kitchen, to fix the shittiness that is this situation. She's at the sink, washing dishes . . . and holding back tears.

I've seen some heartbreaking stuff in my days—but there is nothing on earth more gut-wrenching than watching Chelsea Becker trying her hardest not to cry.

And failing.

I come up behind her, wrap my arms around her waist, and bury my face in her neck.

"I hate this."

She stiffens, and sniffles, but stays silent.

"I fucking hate this. I want you to be happy, but I need to know that you're safe." My arms squeeze tighter. "I won't . . . I won't be able to function if I don't know that. Try and understand. *Please.*"

She gives me more of her weight, leaning back, softening just a little. "I do understand. I would probably feel the same way if things were reversed. But . . . it hurts when you make decisions without me." She hiccups, and it lands like a knife to my stomach. "When you don't think of me."

I turn her around, raising my hands to swipe at her tears with my thumbs. "I do think of you. Always."

Chelsea regards me with wet, wounded eyes and puffy lips. "You should've talked to me about it first, Jake. So it was something we decided together. We're a team . . . remember?"

Her words bring me back to another time, years ago—another argument, and the harsh, stupid words I threw at her. When I was terrified of screwing this up. When I had no fucking clue what I was doing.

Sometimes . . . it feels like I still don't.

"You're right. I'm sorry. I won't do it again, Chelsea." I kiss her gently. Her mouth is warm and soft and yielding. "But you can't keep things from me because you don't like how I'm going to react. I need to know you'll be honest with me."

She nods. "I'm sorry. I was wrong, I should've told you what was going on. I won't keep anything like this from you again. I promise."

What Sofia said yesterday actually did strike a nerve. And although I don't want Chelsea anywhere near that asshole, why the hell should she have to be the one to go?

"Let's go to your HR department today. Together. You don't have to resign. You can file a complaint against Gavin, asked to be moved to another department until your maternity leave starts. Then we can work on getting the son of a bitch fired before you go back after the baby's born."

She stares at my chest thoughtfully. "Okay. I do want to file a complaint, but I'm not going to ask to be moved. Maybe it would be best if I left now—I've been so tired and there's so much to do. And then . . . I think I want to stay home with the baby for a while. Not go back to work right away. For the first year . . . maybe longer?"

I nod. "Sounds like a plan."

When she smiles at me—remorseful and forgiving at the same time—the tightness that's been slowly crushing my chest since yesterday finally loosens. Chelsea's arms wrap around me, holding on tight, and after a few moments every-thing starts to feel normal again.

Our normal is pretty awesome.

Raymond's voice from the doorway, addressing his brothers and sisters, makes us both turn our heads.

"Yeah—they're making out. Divorce averted."

And then . . . we laugh.

# CHAPTER EIGHT

*May*

March and April go by on fast-forward, a blur of plea deals, doctor's appointments, recitals, homework, baseball games . . . and Chelsea's ever-increasing stomach.

It's wild.

She was asleep the first time I felt the baby kick. It was a little before 5 a.m. and my eyes had just opened. I was thinking the ceiling needed to be repainted, when I felt it—a tiny jab against my ribs where the bump pressed against me. It was the first time the reality really hit that there was a baby in there. A whole, new, real, unique little person that Chelsea and I made together. Like I said—fucking wild.

That's when I finally understood what Chelsea felt at that first doctor's appointment. The excitement. Total wonder. And even some impatience.

We decided months ago not to know the baby's sex— much to the kids' deep disappointment. Rory represented his siblings and debated with us for weeks. He cited the delicate boy-girl balance in our household and how the males, in particular, would have to mentally prepare themselves if, as he put it, there wasn't "a penis in there."

I told him there were few real surprises in life, so he was shit out of luck.

Chelsea tried to console him by saying she'd do her best with the penis thing.

But whatever's in there, an auburn-haired little boy or a baby girl who's as beautiful as her mother . . . either way, I can't wait to meet the kid.

———

One early Saturday night, Chelsea and I are watching a movie with three of the kids in the living room, when the front door slams and the sound of sobbing and stomping feet fly up the front stairs.

"Riley?" Chelsea calls, but there's no answer.

So the two of us head to Riley's room. The door that had been taken away from her is now back—and her aunt knocks on it. When all we hear is crying from the other side, we walk in.

Riley's on the floor, her back against her bed, her forehead on her knees. Her cheeks are wet and blotchy and big, heaving sobs rack her shoulders.

Chelsea awkwardly settles on the floor. "Honey?"

Riley looks up. "Peter broke up with me." She pauses to cry into her hand, then goes on. "He said he didn't want a girlfriend during the last summer before college."

"Oh, sweetie." Chelsea envelops Riley in her arms. "I'm so sorry."

I'm not. I'm fucking elated. Best news I've heard all day.

Of course I can't tell Riley that. She wouldn't understand. So I offer my support the only way a guy in this situation possibly can.

"Do you want me to snap him in half for you? It'd be really easy."

Riley squeezes her eyes and shakes her head. "I loved him so much. Why doesn't he love me back?"

Chelsea brushes her niece's hair out of her eyes. And she gets this determined, resolute look on her face. "Listen to me, Riley. Millions of women have been where you are right now. I know it's hard and I know it hurts . . . but I promise you, you will come out of this stronger than you were before. There's a reason; there's something better waiting for you, just around the corner. And it won't hurt like this forever. One day you're going to wake up, take a breath, and realize . . . you're over it. You're over him."

About fifteen minutes later, Riley asks to be alone—so she can listen to depressing songs on repeat and watch YouTube montages about her favorite deceased dystopian-books-made-into-movies characters. As we walk down the hallway, I mention, "You seemed pretty experienced in the whole breakup pep-talk thing."

Her eyes crinkle up at me, curiously. "I've had my share."

"Is that what you thought about me? Back in the day. Were you waiting for the moment when you realized you were over me?"

Boy was that a terrible time. I remember the weeks Chelsea and I spent as civil, polite, platonic friends—at my insistence—with a mixture of shame and nausea.

She wraps her arms around my waist and rests her cheek on my chest. "No. I'd resigned myself to a life of faking it. Because I was sure there was no way . . . I'd ever be over you."

"Yeah. You pretty much ruined me, too, Chelsea."

———

That Tuesday, I'm in the office going over my messages when Brent—and his very round, very pregnant wife—walk in. Kennedy's wearing pink velour sweatpants, one of Brent's Batman T-shirts, and a pair of fuzzy beige boots that probably cost an obscene amount of money. She looks like a homeless person who raided a dumpster in the fashion district.

"Hey, Kennedy."

"Hi, Jake."

"How are you feeling?"

She rubs her protruding belly. "Like a tick ready to pop. Today's my first day of maternity leave."

Her due date is next week.

"Congratulations. What are you doing here?"

She sighs, pushing back a strand of light-blond hair. "I had planned to put my swollen feet up, cuddle with the cats, and reread a Stephenie Meyer novel, but . . ."

Her eyes slide to her husband.

Brent raises his hand guiltily. "I had a dream last night that Kennedy went into labor and I missed the whole thing."

"So he dragged me along with him today."

"You can put your feet up on my office couch. We'll hang out, it'll be great." Brent snaps his fingers and pats his leg, vibrating with more energy than usual.

Kennedy notices, too. "Why don't you go for a run?"

Brent is shocked by the suggestion. "I can't do that. What if your water breaks while I'm gone? I don't want to miss anything."

Kennedy's brown eyes roll to the ceiling. "It's impossible for you to miss anything, Brent! If I stop short you're going to go straight up my ass."

Brent smirks. "Wouldn't be so bad—it's my second favorite place to be."

Kennedy pulls at her hair and she looks to me. "Help."

I shrug. "You married him."

"Seemed like a good idea at the time."

"Knock it off, you two. You're going to hurt my feelings. I'm sensitive."

He says this while walking past me to Stanton's closed office door. He opens it, stands inside for two seconds, and mutters, "O-kay."

Then he turns around and walks back out to the common area. When I try to pass him with a file Stanton was looking for yesterday, he holds up a hand.

"You don't want to go in there, trust me."

I was Stanton's roommate for four years. I know him well—I've seen things.

"What? Are they screwing in there?"

"Yep. In the desk chair." Then he grins. "Did you know Sofia got a tattoo?"

————

An hour later, Stanton and Sofia emerge from the love cave—only slightly red-faced. Which Brent attempts to rectify.

"You dirty dogs . . . what if poor Mrs. Higgens walked in on you?"

Sofia takes a bottle of water out of the minifridge. "Sorry about that."

"Work up a thirst, did you?" I tease.

Stanton slips his tie around his neck and ties it. "Samuel's been coming into our bed at night. Every night. It's made things . . . hard."

Sofia winks.

Stanton gestures to Brent, Kennedy, and me. "See what y'all have to look forward to?"

"Wait a minute," Brent interjects. "Is that like a rule? Are we not supposed to have sex in our offices unless there's a reason?"

His eyes meet Kennedy's. She shrugs. "Oops."

———

I get home late that night—after midnight. The house is dim and quiet; only Cousin It is up to greet me. He hangs out with me on the couch while I eat the plate of food Chelsea left on the stove.

When I walk into our room, I find her stretched out on the bed—awake but tired. She's got one hand on her stomach, peeking out from the snug-fitting tank top, and the other hand holding a thick book.

"Hey." She smiles at me.

"Hey." I loosen my tie and start to unbutton my shirt. "How'd it go tonight?"

"Everybody's good."

I crawl up the bed and kiss her stomach before laying my cheek against the warm, taut skin. "What are you reading?"

She puts the book down and runs her fingers through my hair, rubbing my scalp. "A book on baby names."

"Ahh. Find any good ones?"

Her fingers keep moving and my eyes roll closed under her ministrations.

"I was thinking . . . if we have a little boy . . . we should name him Atticus, after the Judge."

My eyes pop back open, meeting her soft, tender gaze.

"That is a good name."

Chelsea hums her agreement.

I lift my head and press my lips against her stomach again—right next to the belly button that's popped like a well-cooked turkey. "But what do you think about, if it's a boy . . . Robert?"

After her brother. I know it would mean a lot to her—and if it wasn't for him, Chelsea and I wouldn't have met.

Her eyes seem shinier—wet and adoring. "That's a good name, too."

I nod. "And this little one's already going to have a different last name than the rest of the brood—don't want him to feel like an outcast around so many Rs."

"Good point."

"So it's settled then? If it's a boy, he'll be Robert Atticus Becker."

I will never get used to the beauty that is Chelsea's smile.

"I love that," she says softly.

"Me too."

One more kiss later, I drag myself out of the bed and head into the shower.

———

When I walk back into the bedroom, I'm greeted by the sight of my naked wife standing in front of the full-length mirror in the corner, turning left to right—checking herself out.

And damn if my cock doesn't appreciate the view.

"Starting without me?" I tease.

She bites her lip, smiling at me through her reflection in the mirror. "No. I'm just looking." She cocks her head thoughtfully, running her hands up over the mound of her stomach, to her full, heavy breasts. "It's such a strange shape. I'm fine with it, it's temporary, but it's just so . . . odd."

Her suddenly vulnerable blue gaze locks on mine. "Do you still think I'm pretty?"

I can't stop the snort that escapes me. My steps are purposeful as I approach her from behind and press up against her, my hard chest against her delicate spine, my cock sliding between the globes of her supple ass.

A sigh seeps out from my lips, like I'm thinking it over. I sweep the hair from her shoulder and scrape my teeth against the skin of her neck.

"You've never been just pretty, Chelsea. Heart-rippingly stunning—definitely. Unbelievably gorgeous works too."

My palms skim from her hips over her stomach, cupping her tits in a gentle massaging squeeze, then across her collarbone and down her long arms.

Her breathing picks up and her heart thumps in her chest.

I fucking love the way she looks with me pressed against her. The contrast of the colored tattoos that cover my arms against all her pale, smooth, flawless skin. My hand glides back down, coming around her front, resting, then rubbing between her legs.

I groan when I feel her—already slippery and hot. *Fuck*—this woman. It should be terrifying, the way she owns me. But there's too much joy in it . . . to leave any room for fear.

I kiss a trail up her neck to her ear, sucking, nibbling on her lobe.

"Jake . . ." She sighs.

I back up a few steps, taking her with me, until I'm seated on the edge of the bed. I cup one breast in my hand and bring my lips close to its rosy peak, blowing so gently. Then my eyes roll closed as I lick the firm nub. I close my mouth over it, sucking deeply. I could do this for hours—licking her, suckling.

A thought flashes through my mind about what it'll be like after the baby's born. The milk she'll carry—what it'll feel like, taste like. It seems kinky in a way. I've never really been interested in kink. But, goddamn, I could learn.

I release her nipple with a wet pop. And look up into her simmering eyes.

"I want to suck on you until you lose your mind. Then I want you to ride me."

I then spend the whole night showing Chelsea exactly how not-pretty I think she is.

# CHAPTER NINE

*June*

Kennedy goes into labor the first week of June, and she gives birth about a day and a half later. Brent doesn't miss a single second of it. Chelsea and I pay them a visit at the hospital the day after that. Them . . . and their brand-new baby girl.

There's strong hugs and kissed cheeks all around inside the flower-and-pink-balloon-filled room. Kennedy lies in bed, with tired eyes and the sweetest smile I've seen. Brent places a tiny, pink-blanket-wrapped baby in my big hands.

"This is Vivian," he says, total adoration in every syllable.

Chelsea rests her head against my arm, gazing down. "She's so beautiful."

I catch my best friend's eyes—because Vivian sounds familiar.

"You named her after a comic book character, didn't you?"

Kennedy laughs. And Brent shrugs. "Of course. She's extraordinary, so she had to have an extraordinary name. Vivian Rose Victoria Randolph Mason is the long version."

"That's a mouthful."

"She'll get used to it."

"How was the delivery?" Chelsea asks.

She's addressing Kennedy, but Brent beats her to the punch. "Awesome. Don't let anyone scare you, Chelsea. This birthing babies thing is a piece of cake."

Then Kennedy gives the real answer. "Take the drugs, Chelsea. Take *all* the drugs."

———

Two weeks later, I'm in court. Smack-dab in the middle of continuous cross-examination. My phone sits in my pocket, dead as a doornail, because my charger picked this morning to crap out on me. Chelsea is home and still a week from her due date, so I figure it's no big deal. Until the commotion in the back of the courtroom reveals exactly what a big deal it is.

Riley, Rory, Rosaleen, Regan, and Ronan file in, waving their arms and gesturing wildly to me.

"Why are there children in my courtroom?" the cranky judge booms from the bench. "Is this a class trip?"

I raise a finger. "They're mine, Judge."

"All of them?"

"Yes, sir."

"Bring-your-child-to-work day was a few months ago, Mr. Becker."

I watch Rory make a giant arch in front of his stomach, then squeeze his face like he's got a bad case of constipation—and my heart skips three fucking beats.

"My charade skills are rusty, but I'm pretty sure they're here to tell me my wife is in labor."

"Yes! That's it!" Regan yells.

"Shhh!" Rosaleen hisses at her.

"Don't shhh me!"

Rosaleen opens her mouth with a comeback, but the bang of the judge's gavel stops her in her tracks. I should really get a gavel for the house.

"Emergency continuance, Judge?"

He nods. "Granted. Good luck, Mr. Becker—looks like you need it."

As soon as he strikes the gavel again, I'm in front of Riley, her face pale and wild. "Aunt Chelsea is in labor."

Okay, okay—we planned for this. It's not like we didn't know it was coming. My mother's lined up to stay with the kids; Chelsea's bag is packed.

"Is she at the hospital?"

"No, she's home. Raymond's with her. She didn't want to go without you and you weren't answering your phone, so I came to get you. Everyone wanted to come and I didn't want to waste time arguing about it, so I drove the truck."

"You drove the truck?"

Riley has never driven the truck—it's a lot of car for a teenager.

She nods. "I took out two mailboxes on the way here and didn't stop to leave a note. Am I going to get a ticket?"

I take her arm and guide her out the door with the rest of the gang following behind us.

"No—we'll figure it out."

Five minutes later, everyone is buckled in and I'm driving like a NASCAR champion to get to my wife. In the passenger seat, Riley lowers her phone.

"They're still not answering."

"Why the fuck aren't they answering?" I squeeze the steering wheel—only just managing to keep my shit together.

"Why are you guys freaking out?" Rory asks from the backseat.

"Because Aunt Chelsea's having the baby!" Rosaleen snipes.

"So? Chicks have babies every day. What's the big deal?"

Regan joins the conversation. "You're such a moron, Rory."

"Shut up!"

"You shut up!"

"Be. *Quiet*." I don't yell. I don't have to. The steel in my tone snaps all mouths closed.

We pull up to the house fifteen minutes later. I barely get the car in park before I'm sprinting through the front door.

"Chelsea!"

The house is shockingly still. Almost eerily so.

"We're back here!" Raymond calls from my bedroom.

I sense all the kids coming in behind me as I take long, quick strides down the hall. Raymond stands outside our closed bathroom door—ashen and worried.

"Something's wrong, Jake. She keeps saying she's fine but she doesn't sound fine."

I squeeze his shoulder. "Okay, I'm here."

I walk into the bathroom and know right away that Raymond is correct.

Chelsea is definitely not fine.

She sits on the floor, propped up against the wall; her face is colorless and damp with sweat and tears. There's fluid on the ground between her legs and soaked into the hem of her yellow sundress.

She grips the phone tight in her hand when she sees me. And says weakly, "You're here."

I swallow hard. "Yeah, baby, I'm here. Looks like you had a busy morning."

She manages a small laugh, then speaks into the phone. "Yes, my husband, Jake, is here. I'll put him on."

In an instant I'm kneeling next to her. She passes me the phone. "This is Earl. Nine-one-one. I called for an ambulance but there's a water main break so they're going to be a while."

I take the phone but don't bring it to my ear. "I can take you to the hospital now."

Her face pinches in agony and she shakes her head. "I'm sorry. I'm so sorry, Jake. This is all my fault."

"Shhh, it's okay."

"All the books say it takes hours and hours . . . I mean, Kennedy was in labor for two freaking days! So when the contractions started this morning, I thought I could wait until you came home. I knew you were in court . . . I'm such an idiot."

"It's all right, Chelsea."

"Oh God, it hurts. I need to push so bad, Jake. We're not going to make it to the hospital."

I can't tell you why, but I ask, "Are you serious?"

Her face goes hard and furious. "Do I look like I'm fuck-ing *joking*?"

Okay, she's serious.

*Holy shit.*

"Riley, Raymond, Rory—in here now!" I turn on my knees when the three of them stand in the doorway. "Riley . . ."

I don't have to say anything else. She's at Chelsea's side, holding her hand. "Yeah, I'm here."

Tears leak from Chelsea's eyes as she caresses Riley's hair. "You're such a good girl. You always were."

I stand up to talk to the boys. They're stock-still and staring.

"Holy shit!" Rory says. "Is she okay?"

I put my hand on his shoulder. "She's gonna be fine."

He looks up at my face, demanding, "Give me your word."

"You've got it." He nods and I tell him, "Take your brother and sisters out into the living room. Keep them there and keep them calm. Can you do that for me, kid?"

"Yeah—I'm on it." He glances around me. "I love you, Aunt Chelsea."

Chelsea smiles, despite her obvious pain. "I love you, too, Rory. Don't worry."

With a nod, he leaves.

I wrap one hand around Raymond's arm, bringing his attention to me. "Your aunt is having the baby."

"Here?!"

"Here. Now. And I really need you not to freak out about it, Raymond. Bring me towels, scissors, string. Then boil some water, just in case."

From what I read, the boiling water is for sterilizing things, and I don't think we're going to have time for that. But it'll keep Raymond busy so he doesn't worry himself sick.

I give his arm another squeeze. "Are you with me?"

His face tightens with determination. "Yeah. We got this."

"Atta boy."

I let myself take one last big breath as he leaves. Then I kneel back down beside Chelsea. From the living room, I can hear the little kids crying. Arguing. Calling for her.

Chelsea hears it, too.

"Riley," I say, "go help Rory with the kids. I've got things here."

For a moment she looks unsure. Then she kisses Chelsea's cheek and goes.

Chelsea looks up at me, and my heart feels like it's imploding.

"Hey."

"Alone at last." I say in my calmest voice. I tilt my head toward the phone on the floor. "Well . . . except for Earl."

That gets me a tiny smile. And even more tears. "I'm really scared, Jake."

I shake my head. "I know you are, but you don't have to be. I'm not going to let anything happen to you or this baby."

"This isn't what we planned."

I cup her beautiful face in both hands. "I didn't plan on you, Chelsea. Or them. And for as long as I live, you will be the best thing that ever happened to me."

She closes her eyes and leans into my palm.

"We're gonna have a baby today. And we're gonna have one fuck of a story afterward. Okay?"

She takes one of her deep breaths, and that face that I love turns focused. Strong. Determined—like she's always been.

"Okay."

I put the phone on speaker. "This is Jake Becker—are you there, Earl?"

"I'm here, Jake." A gravelly, older man's voice comes out of the speaker. It reminds me so much of the Judge, I blink. "I'm going to walk you through this every step of the way, son."

"Sounds good."

"Okay. First, take a look and tell me what's going on."

Chelsea's underwear is already off. I grab a towel from the stack that Raymond dropped in the room and place it underneath her. Then I put my hands on her knees and look between her legs.

*Holy fucking Christ*

There's a mass of dark hair that I know isn't hers, pushing against her opening, stretching her. "I see the head. It's inside her still, but it's right there."

"That's good. I want you to wash your hands now, Jake, get some clean towels nearby, and get ready to catch."

I scrub and dry my hands, then Chelsea groans deep and loud. "Oh God, I have to push. I have to right now."

I tell Earl I'm ready and he says, "Go ahead, Chelsea. A few good pushes and you'll be meeting your baby. Breathe deep and focus, okay? Your body knows what it needs to do, don't fight it, let it happen."

Chelsea grips her knees and curls her spine. Her chin drops to her chest and she growls as she bears down hard.

And while I wait between Chelsea's legs, I silently do something I've never done before.

I pray.

I go back and forth between cursing God, telling him he can't have her—to threatening that if he tries, I'll march straight into heaven, scoop Chelsea up, and carry her home. But mostly, I just beg.

*Please, God, please don't let me screw this up. Don't let anything go wrong. Please, God, please, please, please, fucking* **please***.*

And then my voice is echoing off the walls. "The head is out."

My child's face is still, covered in fluid and splotched with a white fleshy substance.

"It's not over!" Chelsea grunts and strains even harder.

And then, in a rush of liquid, my son slides into my hands.

"He's out!" I call. I grab a towel and wipe his face, clearing his nose and mouth.

"Is he crying?" Earl asks.

The answer is a strong, pissed-off screech. And it's the most beautiful fucking sound I've ever heard.

"Yeah, he is. He's crying."

And he's not the only one.

His little mouth opens wide and indignant. His tiny, perfect limbs flail as I dry them with the towel. His sounds change to whimpers as I wrap him up in a new, dry towel and put him on Chelsea's stomach. In her arms.

She cries as she holds him, looks at him. And her whisper is feather soft. "Hi, there. We've all been waiting for you."

I lean down next to her and rest my forehead against her temple—just breathing her in. Holding them both close.

"We did it, Jake."

*Thank you, thank you, thank you . . .*

"We sure did."

———

Talk about a fucking day.

The paramedics showed up a few minutes after Robert was born. They took care of the umbilical cord, and Chelsea, and all the things that need to happen right after childbirth. Each of the kids got a good look at Robert before he and Chelsea were loaded into the ambulance. The boys were thrilled to have a new little brother, and the girls decided he was so damn cute, they didn't even mind that he had a penis.

Stanton and Sofia stayed with them while I rode with Chelsea. Mother and baby stayed overnight, just to make sure everybody was good to go. When they came home, we let the kids take off from school for the rest of the week—which is always a cause for celebration.

We're all lying around the den now, watching TV in our pajamas, even though it's two o'clock in the afternoon. A pitiful cry from the baby monitor tells us that someone is up, probably wet and hungry. I kiss Chelsea—it's like I'm unable not to kiss her—every time the baby cries. Which is a lot.

"I'll get him," I say against her sweet mouth.

Down the hall, in our room, I lift him from the bassinet and change his diaper. And he really doesn't like that. I swaddle him back up and sit in the rocking chair, soothing him.

His whimpers die down and he just kind of looks at me, the way babies do—like he's waiting for something. After a few seconds, I think maybe he wants a song—a lullaby. There's one band that gets played in this house more than any other, so against my better judgment, it's one of their songs I choose.

I sing in a low, off-key voice . . . until the sound of a lone giggle floats down the hall and under the door. Then it's joined by another.

And another.

Until there's a full-blown chorus of chuckles going on in the living room.

And Regan's high-pitched voice informs me, "We can hear you singing One Direction!"

That's when I remember . . . the fucking baby monitor. I shake my head and laugh at myself. Then I look down into my son's dark, pensive gaze.

"We're never going to live this one down. Ever."

# EPILOGUE

*Seventeen years later*

I'm working from home today—because if I've learned anything after raising kids, it's the moment you let your guard down, the second you make plans that don't revolve around them, they screw with you.

I'm at my desk, halfway through the final read-through of a motion for dismissal, when the door opens, and Chelsea pops her head in. She's every bit as hot in her late forties as the day she opened that front door and literally took my breath away. I'm a lucky bastard.

"It's time, Jake."

I stand up, grab my jacket from the back of my chair, and follow her out. We stop in the den, where Robert and Vivian are stretched out on the couch, watching TV and feeding each other popcorn. They've been a couple since middle school—it's not really that surprising since they were practically attached at the hip before they were even born.

I don't know if they'll be together for eternity, like they say they will. They're young, and life is so very unpredictable. But I know they'll be friends for the rest of their lives.

"Your mother and I are going to the hospital. Are you coming?"

My son takes after me in build and personality. He's stubborn and rebellious, but there's a playfulness to him that I never had—because his childhood was a hell of a lot different from my own. And I'll never stop being grateful for that. He has his mother's eyes and her steely but kind resilience. I'm grateful for that, too.

He shakes his dark head. "Nah, but call me after the baby's born—we'll come then."

I take three steps toward the front door, stop, and turn around. "Don't screw around while we're out of the house."

It might seem like an awkward thing to say to my kid—and it is. But I'm a realist, and believe it or not, so are teenagers.

Vivian grins mischievously. "Come on, Uncle Jake—would we do that?"

Vivian is the spitting image of her mother—tiny and pretty, with golden-brown eyes that glow with a soft inner light. But her personality is all her father. And I've known Brent Mason for thirty years.

"Yes. You would totally do that."

She giggles and buries her face in my son's shoulder. I point my finger at him. "But don't. Seriously. Ronan's on his way back from school—he can come home at any minute."

Robert holds up a placating palm. "Relax, Dad. It's all good. Tell Rory and Lori I said good luck."

From the doorway, Chelsea says, "See you later, kids. There's juice in the fridge."

As we walk down the front steps, my brow furrows at my wife. "Juice? Did you just meet those two? We should be locking down the fucking liquor cabinet."

She shrugs. "The real stuff is hidden in our closet; I replaced all the bottles in the cabinet with water months ago. If they're in the mood for a cocktail, they're going to be disappointed."

God, I love this woman. "Well played."

She pokes my ribs. "This is not my first rodeo, Mr. Becker."

———

At the hospital, Chelsea and I sit in the waiting room of the maternity floor, drinking bad coffee. Lori's parents head down to the cafeteria, and about fifteen minutes after they go, Rory McQuaid comes barreling through the double doors, his expression tired but completely elated.

"It's a boy!"

Chelsea squeaks, jumps up, and tackles her nephew. And my smile is so broad, my cheeks ache. After Chelsea eventually relinquishes her hold, I give a back-slapping bear hug of my own.

"I'm proud of you, kid."

Rory smirks the same smirk that changed my life.

"Thanks. I'm pretty proud of me, too."

"How's Lori?" Chelsea asks.

"She's great. You guys can come back—they're ready for visitors."

We follow him into the cheery hospital room, where his wife reclines against a mountain of pillows. Lori grins when we walk in, her cheeks joyously round. She's a high school teacher—and so gorgeous she must have to beat those teen-age bastards off with a bat. Rory met her when she was a character witness for one of her students—who was also Rory's client. It wasn't love at first sight—but it was damn close.

Yeah, Rory is a criminal defense attorney at my firm. He's sharp, committed, tough—and he has a partiality for defending juvenile cases. He's not a partner; hasn't gotten McQuaid added to the firm name just yet . . . but I have no doubt in a few years, he will.

I kiss Lori's cheek. "Congratulations, sweetheart."

"Thanks, Jake."

Chelsea lifts the sleeping bundle of baby from the bassinet. She gazes down at him with so much love and sighs, "Oh, honey . . . he's beautiful. He looks just like you, Rory."

Lori teases, "We're really hoping he takes after me personality-wise."

I tap Rory's shoulder. "Karma's a bitch."

He nods, chuckling.

I stand next to Chelsea and look at the baby in her arms. Smooth skin, long dark lashes, fucking adorable little face. Now this—this is love at first sight.

"Hi, baby," Chelsea coos. "I'm your grandma."

Gran-MILF is what I like to call her. Weird . . . but so true.

"Do you have a name for him yet?" she asks.

Lori glances at Rory—a special, secret kind of look. "We do. We've had it for a while now. Rory picked it and I thought it was perfect."

When they don't say anything else, I ask, "Are you gonna tell us or do we have to guess?"

Rory looks up into my eyes. And says quietly, "Becker. My son's name is Becker McQuaid."

I stare back at him, until my eyes start to burn. And I just know Chelsea is tearing up next to me. I look down at the baby again, through a blurry gaze.

Then I walk up to Rory, clearing my throat. "You're gonna make me cry, you little shit."

His mouth quirks. "That was my evil plan all along, old man."

I hug him. Hold him tight—because I'm honored.

"Thank you, Rory."

He hugs me back and says against my ear, "Thank *you*, Jake. For everything."

A few minutes later, Lori's parents come in—then Regan and Ronan show up, bickering about the route Ronan drove to get them here. Not long after that, the whole brood descends, to welcome our newest addition.

———

Are you wondering about the others? Where they are, how they turned out? Today's your lucky day, because I'm going I'll tell you.

Riley lives in LA. She started her own business—party planner to the stars. She's not married, but she's been living with the same guy for the last ten years. Considering I moved my ass in with her aunt before we were married, Chelsea and I had a whole lot of nothing to say about that. The guy's . . . okay. I don't hate him—wouldn't say I like him, either. He makes Riley happy, so, at least for now, I won't have to kill him.

I'd like to tell you that Raymond's first crush dream came true—that he and Presley Sunshine Shaw dated, fell in love, and lived happily ever after. But they didn't.

Turned out, four years—in teen years—was just too big of a hurdle to climb.

Presley became an attorney, like her father—and she married a lawyer, also like her dad. They live just over the Virginia state line, on a horse farm that reminds Stanton of his parents' place in Mississippi.

Raymond ended up majoring in computer science—no surprise there. His last year of college, he did an internship with a bunch of other brainiacs in Silicon Valley. One of his fellow internshippers was a pretty little thing with dark hair and big brown eyes, who thinks Raymond hung the moon. She said he was the first man she ever met who was smarter than she was. I'm still getting used to the idea of someone referring to Raymond as a man—not sure when that happened. They've been married about two years now, and the only thing that gets them more charged up than a new iPhone is each other.

Rosaleen followed in the footsteps of her mother, Rachel. She married her college sweetheart and started having kids not long after. She's got three little girls and counting. They're bouncy, blond, and beautiful and remind me so much of her, it hurts. Her husband's a well-paid campaign consultant and they live only a couple miles away in a house bigger than ours.

Regan is a speech therapist in Alexandria. She just finished her graduate degree and shares an apartment with her best friend from high school. She's young and gorgeous and having a good time dating every guy she meets. She swears she'll never settle down because she'll never find a guy who can measure up to me.

Can't really argue with that logic.

Little Ronan isn't so little anymore. He's twenty-two and just finished the pre-med program at Georgetown. Next up is medical school—and he wants to specialize in obstetrics. Sometimes Chelsea and I wonder how big of an impact Robert's bathroom home birth had on Ronan. Neither of us asks because we don't really want to know the answer.

Whoever said "you can't go home again" never had a family. Because even though they're grown, with lives of their own, and are spread out all over the country—our kids come home all the time. At Christmas and Easter the house is fucking bursting.

I grumble that it's a pain in the ass. I complain about the craziness and noise and the chaos. Chelsea just laughs at me.

She says, I love it—that I wouldn't change a single thing.

And . . . she's right.

# BONUS MATERIAL

Keep reading for a special treat!

What follows is a chapter that ended up getting deleted from the final version of *Appealed,* but I'm excited to share it with you now! No spoilers if you haven't read *Appealed* yet.

Enjoy!

~Emma

*Brent & Kennedy – 11 years old*

They sat beside each other on the rocks along the water, after sharing the lunch she had stuffed in her backpack—spitting black watermelon seeds into the water.

"So you don't remember anything?"

*Woothoo*

Kennedy's seed flew from her mouth and landed close to shore. As far as spitting distance went—hers was pathetic.

"Nope. Not the day of the accident or the three days before it. It's just gone."

It had been two years since Brent's accident. They hadn't seen each other the first year—after his long hospital stay there'd been too many doctor appointments and physical therapy sessions. This was the first time they'd talked about "the tragedy," as Kennedy's parents called it.

"That must feel strange."

*Woothoo*

"Yeah. But my doctors said it's normal—head injury, the shock from bleeding so much."

"What happened to the guy who hit you?"

Brent shrugged. And spit. *Woothoo.* "My parents wanted him to go to jail. Our lawyers argued with the police because they didn't give him a ticket. But they said he wasn't speeding, wasn't drunk. He didn't see me coming around the bend and I didn't see him."

"And you're okay with that?"

"I am now. I talked about it with my therapist. Sometimes stuff just happens. And it's no one's fault."

"Your therapist? Like a psychiatrist?"

"Yeah."

*Woothoo*

"What's that like?"

"Weird." Brent thought for a moment, then added. "But in a good way. My mother insisted on it, said I had to work through the trauma. But I think she's more traumatized than I am. She says I'm not allowed to ride a bike again—ever. She had them removed from all the houses and gave them to charity. Even the stationery ones."

"Like Sleeping Beauty."

"What?" Brent asked.

"Sleeping Beauty. A curse was cast on her that she would prick her finger on a spinning wheel when she was sixteen and fall into a coma. So her parents banned all the spinning wheels from the kingdom to keep her safe." She patted his head and teased, "You're just like Aurora."

He frowned. "If you start calling me Aurora, I'm going to start calling you Speck because you're so short."

Kennedy nudged him playfully, and spit another seed—missing the water entirely.

Brent shook his head. "You spit like a girl."

Kennedy turned towards him, and launched a seed at his forehead. This one was a direct hit.

"Like an awesome girl." She corrected.

Brent chuckled and wiped his forehead. "Anyway, I'm not Sleeping Beauty and I really miss my bike." Then he squinted at the sun. "It's getting late. I gotta go—my mother breaks out in hives if I'm out of the house too long."

Kennedy watched Brent as he stood and gathered his lacrosse stick and his bucket of balls. And then she had an idea.

"Hey—do you know that field in the woods—the one that used to be an Indian burial ground?"

All the children who grew up in the area knew about it—and most stayed away. Satanic rituals were rumored to be held there.

"Yeah, what about it?"

Kennedy's top row of braces scraped across her bottom lip as her quick mind outlined a plan. "Meet me there tomorrow."

———

*The Next Day*

"What is that?" Brent asked, eyeing the contraption Kennedy stood beside.

"It's a bike."

"It's pink." Brent pointed out. "Really pink."

"It's a bike." Kennedy repeated, firmer this time.

"It has streamers."

"It has wheels," Kennedy replied. "And you're going to ride it."

Brent walked closer to the girly nightmare. The memory of coasting down hills, popping wheelies, and jumping over curbs made his pulse quicken. They were things he never thought he'd be able to do again—things his parents would have a heart attack about if he did.

"I don't know if I can do this, Kennedy."

Her soft brown eyes looked up at him. "Of course you can."

"But what if I can't? Like, anymore?"

Kennedy gently touched Brent's wrist. "If you really want to, you will."

She sounded so certain, he believed her.

Brent swung his right leg over the small bike, awkwardly, hopping a bit on his prosthetic. He gripped the handle bars and tried to raise the kickstand. It took him three tries, but he did it. Then he sat on the bike, braced his prosthetic foot on the pedal and pushed. It slipped off before he moved an inch. He repositioned himself and tried again, but his balance was all wrong and he was just able to catch himself before he toppled over.

"This is gonna take a while," he said, then sighed.

Kennedy sat on the ground and folded her hands around her knees. "We've got all summer."

———

*One Week Later*

"Woooooo! Faster Brent!"

Kennedy's brown braid had come loose and her hair tickled his face, lifted by the wind that poured over them as they raced down the hill. She sat on the handlebars, her feet braced on the lip of the bolt on either side of the wheel. Brent stood behind her, pumping the pedals.

"Okay—hold on!"

And they were off. He flew down the path, through shadows and patches of sun, bouncing over roots and rocks, thin branches slapping at his arms, still wet from yesterday's rain, but he didn't feel the sting. Because he was having too much fun. It felt like he was flying.

And he felt something else he hadn't for a long time. Normal.

"Yes!" Kennedy screeched. "Go-go gadget leg!"

Brent laughed, ducking his head beneath a particularly low branch. Then he pulled up on the handlebars to hop over a raised bump, making her bounce.

He was having such a good time, he didn't notice the large rock right in the bike's path.

Not until they'd hit it.

And then he was literally flying—they both were. His breath burst from his lungs as he landed in the wet grass with a hard grunt. For a second, he didn't move. Nothing felt broken or injured. Then he sat up. Brent saw the bike on its side a few feet away, the back tire still spinning. He saw Kennedy a few feet beyond that. Her glasses had been knocked off her face, her eyes were closed and she wasn't moving.

At all.

As he looked at her, something inside him felt like it was breaking after all. In the seconds it took to get to her, a dozen thoughts ran through his head—each more horrible than the one before.

She was hurt—and it was all his fault. He would never forgive himself.

Never.

"Kennedy!" He knelt beside her, touching her cheek, looking for blood, his voice raw. "Kennedy wake up! Look at me."

Instantly her eyes snapped open, shining like amber stones. And Brent was so relieved, he didn't realize what was happening.

Not until Kennedy said, "Gotcha!"

Then she laughed. Loudly. Freely. Without a worry in the world.

Brent sat back. Relief turned to understanding. And understanding turned to anger. "You idiot! You scared the crap out of me."

Disgusted, he scrambled to his feet and walked a few steps away.

"You should've seen your face!" Kennedy cackled.

Then she slipped her glasses on and was able to see what Brent's face actually looked like. Pale. Tight. His breath escaped fast and hard.

Then she wasn't laughing anymore. Because she realized what she hadn't before: Bad things, terrible things really did happen. And Brent knew that better than anyone—because they had happened to him.

The smile fell from her lips. She crawled forward, rose to her knees. "Brent, I'm sorry. I didn't think . . . it was stupid. I'm really sorry."

He didn't look at her right away. He stood, turned around, his hands on his hips.

And Kennedy wanted to cry. She could do it, easily, because she felt so awful.

When he did finally face her, his eyes were hard, two sharp-cut sapphires. Then he forced out a big breath. "It was stupid. And do you know what happens to stupid girls?"

"What?"

"They get the mud."

Kennedy wasn't familiar with that expression. But as she started to ask what the heck he was talking about, a glob of cold, wet mud landed on her shirt—splattering across her chest and neck.

"Ah!" She yelled out.

She looked between her muddy shirt and the boy who'd made it that way. And he was smiling again.

Kennedy's eyes narrowed. "You are so dead."

She scooped up the wet earth and formed a ball in her hand, like a mucky snowball.

Brent wiggled his muddy fingers at her. "Oooh, I'm so scared."

Kennedy Randolph didn't just spit like a girl—she threw like one too.

A girl with perfect aim.

Brent tried to dodge the attack, but a moment later the back of his white t-shirt resembled the Rorschach Test. And it was on. They scrambled and crawled, flung and smeared, screamed and shouted and trash talked. When it was over, there wasn't a clean spot between the two of them. Brent spit brown saliva. Kennedy used a leaf to wipe off her glasses.

"If my mother saw me right now, she'd shite bricks."

"What?" Brent laughed.

"Seamus, our new driver is Irish. That's how he says the s-word—shite. I like the way it sounds. Shite bricks. It makes me feel powerful."

Brent fell on his back, still laughing. "You're crazy, you know that?"

Kennedy shrugged. "I'd rather be crazy than boring." Then she smacked Brent's leg – leaving a muddy handprint behind. "Let's ride down to the river and clean up."

Brent sobered as they stood and walked toward the bike. "Maybe we shouldn't ride anymore."

"Why not?"

"We could fall again. You might get hurt, Kennedy."

The small girl turned to him, hands on her hips, stubbornness in her jaw. "We probably will fall again—and that's why we have to get back on and keep riding. The ride is the only thing that makes falling worth it."

Brent squinted. "Okay, human fortune cookie."

Kennedy stuck her tongue out at him. "Don't be such a pussycat."

He just looked at her blankly. "What the heck does that mean?"

"I heard Seamus say it to the gardener. He said, 'Don't be a pussy,'" She shrugged. "I think he meant pussycat, like 'Don't be a chicken.'"

"I don't think Seamus is gonna be your driver for very long," Brent said before reluctantly climbing on the bike with Kennedy on the handle bars.

He rode slower at first, but when she begged him to go faster, he did.

Because he was no pussycat.

———

*Three Weeks Later*

They were by the pool. Mrs. Mason hyperventilated when the Mason's butler, Henderson, caught them swimming in the river—even though Brent's physical therapist said his prosthetic was saltwater grade. She made him promise that the only place he'd swim was here at the pool, with Henderson close by. There wasn't anything Brent hated more than seeing his mother upset, so he made a promise—and stuck to it.

So, they were poolside, in the shade of a cherry tree, on two huge cotton towels. Brent liked the pool better anyway— he could swim without his leg, without crawling through the rocky sand to retrieve it, or worrying that it'd be washed away and sink to the bottom of the Potomac River. That would suck.

But he wasn't swimming now. And Kennedy knew he wasn't listening either.

Because he was on his back, shirtless and tan, damp hair curving over his forehead, one arm bent behind his head, the other holding a comic book. He always had one with him—in his back pocket. And if they weren't doing something that required movement, Brent was reading.

"I'm going to shave my head. What do you think about that?" Kennedy asked.

"Cool."

"And then I'm going to steal a car. Get a tattoo. Change my name to Snowflake."

"Uh huh."

Her hair fell over the strap of her green bathing suit as she leaned towards him. "Then I'm going to sneak into your room, take everything you own and sell it at the flea market."

"That's nice."

Kennedy rolled her eyes. And pinched Brent's bicep.

"Ow! What'd you do that for?"

She waited for him to look at her. Then she asked, "What's with the comic books?"

Brent shrugged. "They're cool." Then he tried to go back to reading.

*Tried.*

Kennedy snatched the comic from his hands and flipped through the pages. Brent turned on his side, bracing his head on his hand.

"Why are all the girls in bikinis?" She looked more closely and added, "Barely."

Brent chuckled. "That's just how they draw them."

"Is that why you think they're cool?"

"That's not the only reason," he hedged.

She adjusted her glasses, waiting for him to continue. Eventually, he did.

"Right after the accident, I couldn't do anything. Couldn't even get out of bed to take a wizz. It drove me nuts. So my father started bringing me stuff to read. Books were too long, I'd fall asleep from the medicine after a few pages. But comics were quick and it was easy to pick up where I'd left off when I woke up. Two weeks after the accident, he bought me Superman #1. Do you know what that is?"

"No."

"It's one of the rarest comic books in the world—worth like, a million dollars. It was wrapped in plastic because that keeps it valuable. My father showed it to me, then tore the plastic right off, because he said being able to watch me read it was worth more than a million dollars."

"That's awesome." Kennedy said breathlessly. She couldn't imagine her mother being content to watch her read anything—not without telling her she was doing it wrong. "So that's why you read them all the time, because your father bought you your first one?"

Brent shook his head. "That's why I started, but I keep reading them because . . . because all the heroes had something bad happen. Really bad. And it . . . changed them. But they weren't just different afterwards, they were better. More than they ever could've been if the bad thing hadn't happened, you know?"

Kennedy nodded.

"That's how I want to be too."

Kennedy handed him back his comic book and smiled. "I think you already are."

After a quiet moment, she asked, "Is that what you want to do, for your career when you're older? Collect rare comic books? My Uncle Edgar collects Egyptian artifacts for a living. He smells weird."

"No, I don't want to do that. Drawing comic books would be an awesome job, but I suck at drawing. What do you want to do when you get older?"

Kennedy thought about it. "Truth?" she asked him.

"Truth."

She leaned closer. "I want to do . . . whatever my mother doesn't want me to."

*Four Weeks Later*

They were working on their ladder. Prosthetic leg or not, Brent couldn't climb trees like he used to—and there were a lot of good climbing trees on the acres between their houses. So they'd decided to build a ladder. A good one. A tall one. One that would get him to the highest branch.

And if they had time, Kennedy wanted to build a hut, like the Ewoks in *Return of the Jedi*. They'd watched the movie in her home theater the other day during a thunderstorm.

Thinking of the movie made her think of where she'd had to go after the movie—to her final dress fitting. For the dress her mother commissioned for Claire's party. The party that was one week away.

"Are you coming to Claire's graduation party?" she asked.

Brent took the nail out of his mouth, lined it up, and pounded it into the wood in two quick strikes. "I don't know. My parents are."

"Of course your parents are coming. That's not what I asked."

He stopped and looked at her, his face serious. Kennedy didn't like it—it made him look not like Brent. Because her Brent was never serious.

"I don't think so."

Kennedy put down the saw and moved closer to him. "Why not?"

Now there was sadness in those round blue eyes.

And it was all wrong.

"I think . . . I think they're embarrassed of me, Kennedy."

Anger sparked inside her, quick and hot. "Did they say that to you?"

Brent shook his head. "No, just a feeling, you know?"

The anger fizzled, but only a little. "Your parents love you, Brent."

He nodded. "I know. But you can love something and still be ashamed of it, can't you?"

And that was true. She couldn't lie to him, because it was the story of her life. All she could do was let him know he wasn't alone. "Then you should definitely come to the party. My mother's ashamed of me all the time."

The sadness in his eyes lightened, and he gave her a small smile. Then he put his hand over hers and squeezed.

———

The party was perfect—exactly as her mother planned. A full orchestra filled the night air with elegant music, pristine white tents covered tables with overflowing centerpieces, fine china and high backed chairs. White gloved waiters were everywhere, their trays laden with champagne flutes, caviar and oysters. There was a constant hum of conversation among the hundreds of guests—anyone who was anyone was in attendance. The flash of the photographers' cameras burst like fireflies on a dark night. Recording these moments for posterity, making the guests feel like they were worthy of their very own paparazzi. And in the center of it all was Claire Randolph, her long blond hair shimmering, her pale yellow ball gown not fit for a princess—but for a queen.

Kennedy was bored out of her mind.

She sat at a table, alone, a small smile plastered in place, because, as her mother had warned her—unsmiling young ladies looked sullen. Sullen equaled pouty. And pouting was never allowed.

At eleven, she was the youngest here—the only girl still considered a child—because none of the other guests would entertain bringing children to such an affair. She was too young to drink, too full to eat more, too uninteresting to engage in conversation for long.

But as she gazed through her glasses at the crowd, she saw him—standing beside his parents, looking as handsome as a prince in a sharp tuxedo. Brent had come—he would save her from the boredom monster. Kennedy darted out of her chair and walked straight to him.

"Hello, Kennedy." His father greeted in his familiar rough, deep voice.

"Hello, Mr. Mason."

Brent's mother, always soft and sweet, smiled genuinely and Kennedy smiled back. Then her eyes fixed on her friend. His hands were folded behind his back, his eyes scanned the room—not nervous—but cautious. Careful not to do the wrong thing.

"Hey."

His blue eyes warmed when they rested on her.

"Hey. You look nice."

She shrugged. "Thanks." Then she leaned closer, so only he could hear. "Do you want to dance? There's nothing else to do."

Brent knew a few ballroom dances—his mother had taught him, to help him become the refined gentleman they all expected him to be. But he hadn't even thought to try them in public—not since the accident.

"I might trip."

Kennedy reached out her hand. "Then I'll catch you."

"Yeah, right. I would squash you." He snorted.

She shook her head. "I'm stronger than I look."

He held her eyes for a few seconds. Then Brent took her hand and led her to the dance floor.

It was a basic waltz, a simple box step. And Brent didn't trip.

They talked as they danced, and laughed.

Neither of them saw Brent's mother's eyes fill with tears or his father's fill with pride. Because although a tragedy had befallen their dear son, they knew then that his life would not be tragic.

———

Kennedy and Brent were inseparable for the remainder of that summer. And even after school began again in the fall—with Kennedy back at her all girls day academy and Brent at home with his tutors—they saw each other at least once a week. When the next summer came around, they were inseparable again.

Brent thought of them as a dynamic duo—like Batman and Robin or Green Arrow and Speedy. Kennedy imagined they were more like Winnie Cooper and Kevin Arnold.

She thought they would be best friends forever.

But...she was wrong.

They'd become so much more.

OTHER BOOKS BY

EMMA CHASE

# THE TANGLED SERIES

### Tangled

*In Emma Chase's sizzling and hilarious debut novel, Drew Evans—gorgeous, arrogant, irreverent, and irresistibly charming—meets his match in new colleague Kate Brooks.*

Drew Evans is handsome and arrogant, he makes multimillion dollar business deals and seduces New York's most beautiful women with just a smile. So why has he been shuttered in his apartment for seven days, miserable and depressed? He'll tell you he has the flu. But we all know that's not really true.

Katherine Brooks is brilliant, beautiful and ambitious. When Kate is hired as the new associate at Drew's father's investment banking firm, every aspect of the dashing playboy's life is thrown into a tailspin. The professional competition she brings is unnerving, his attraction to her is distracting, his failure to entice her into his bed is exasperating.

*Tangled* is not your mother's romance novel. It is an outrageous, passionate, witty narrative about a man who knows a lot about women...just not as much as he thinks. As he tells his story, Drew learns the one thing he never wanted in life, is the only thing he can't live without.

### Twisted

*Falling in love is easy. Staying in love is hard. In this heart-pounding follow-up to Tangled, Kate reveals that there is trouble in paradise, when unexpected circumstances force her and Drew to "renegotiate" their relationship.*

There are two kinds of people in the world. The ones who look first, and the ones who leap. I've always been more of a looker. Cautious. A planner. That changed after I met Drew Evans. He was so persistent. So sure of himself—and of me.

But not all love stories end happily ever after. Did you think Drew and I were going to ride off into the sunset? Join the club. Now I have to make a choice; the most important of my life. Drew already made his—in fact, he tried to decide for the both of us. But you know that's just not my style. So I came back to Greenville, Ohio, alone. Well, sort of alone...

What I've come to realize is that old habits die hard, and sometimes you have to go back to where you began before you can move ahead.

### Tamed

*Matthew Fisher—the best friend of Drew Evans from Tangled and Twisted—wants to settle down, but he'll have to overcome the mistrust of the colorful and unique Dee Dee Warren.*

Stop me if you've heard this one before: girl meets player, they fall in love, player changes his ways.

It's a good story. But it's not our story. Ours is a lot more colorful.

When I met Dee, I knew right away that she was special. When she met me, she thought I was anything *but* special—I was exactly like every other guy who'd screwed her over and let her down. It took some time to convince her otherwise, but it turns out I can make a convincing argument when sex is at stake.

You might know where this story's headed. But the best part isn't where we ended up.

It's how we got there.

### Tied

*In the fourth sexy romance in the Tangled Series, Drew and Kate can't wait to tie the knot—if they can survive the pre-wedding festivities.*

For most of my life, I never imagined I'd get married. But Kate did the impossible: she changed me. I think we can all agree I was pretty frigging awesome before, but now I'm even better.

The road to this day wasn't all rainbows and boners. There were mistakes and misunderstandings worthy of a Greek tragedy. But Kate and I made it through with our inexhaustible lust, boundless admiration, and everlasting love for one another intact.

That being said, there were some unexpected incidents in Vegas last weekend that could have been a problem. It was kind of...my final test.

I know what you're thinking—*what the hell did you do this time?* Relax. Let's not judge, or call for my castration, until you've heard the whole story.

And hold on tight, because you're in for a wild ride. Did you expect anything less?

## "Holy Frigging Matrimony"
*What does Drew Evans have to say next? Find out in this short story, filled with his sexy charm, unique advice and hilarious one-liners.*

Marriage: the final frontier. Steven went first. He was kind of our test subject. Like those monkeys that NASA sent off into space in the fifties, all the while knowing they'd never make it back.

And now another poor rocket is ready to launch.

But this isn't just any posh New York wedding. You've seen my friends, you've met our families, you know you're in for a treat. Everyone wants their wedding to be memorable. This one's going to be un-frigging-forgettable.

## "It's a Wonderful Tangled Christmas Carol"
*Drew and Kate play a hilarious encore to* Tangled *in this sexy take on A Christmas Carol, in which three dream women remind Drew that no gift could be better than his life with Kate...*

After a blowout fight with Kate about his workaholic habits sends Drew to the office in anger on Christmas Eve, he falls asleep at his desk. There, three lovely holiday spirits magically visit him to teach him that every moment is precious and that he should never take his family for granted. But when he wakes up, will he just write it off as a dream?

# THE LEGAL BRIEFS SERIES

### Overruled

A Washington, DC, defense attorney, Stanton Shaw keeps his head cool, his questions sharp, and his arguments irrefutable. They don't call him the Jury Charmer for nothing—with his southern drawl, disarming smile, and captivating green eyes, he's a hard man to say no to. Men want to be him, and women want to be thoroughly cross examined by him.

Stanton's a man with a plan. And for a while, life was going according to that plan.

Until the day he receives an invitation to the wedding of his high school sweetheart, the mother of his beloved ten-year-old daughter. Jenny is getting married—to someone who isn't him.

That's definitely not part of the plan. Sofia Santos is a city-raised, no-nonsense litigator who plans to become the most revered criminal defense attorney in the country. She doesn't have time for relationships or distractions.

But when Stanton, her "friend with mind-blowing benefits," begs her for help, she finds herself out of her element, out of her depth, and obviously out of her mind. Because she agrees to go with him to The-Middle-Of-Nowhere,

Mississippi, to do all she can to help Stanton win back the woman he loves. Her head tells her she's crazy...and her heart says something else entirely.

What happens when you mix a one-stop-light town, two professional arguers, a homecoming queen, four big brothers, some Jimmy Dean sausage, and a gun-toting Nana?

The Bourbon flows, passions rise, and even the best-laid plans get overruled by the desires of the heart.

### Sustained

When you're a defense attorney in Washington, DC, you see firsthand how hard life can be, and that sometimes the only way to survive is to be harder. I, Jake Becker, have a reputation for being cold, callous, and intimidating—and that suits me just fine. In fact, it's necessary when I'm breaking down a witness on the stand.

Complications don't work for me—I'm a "need-to-know" type of man. If you're my client, tell me the basic facts. If you're my date, stick to what will turn you on. I'm not a therapist or Prince Charming—and I don't pretend to be.

Then Chelsea McQuaid and her six orphaned nieces and nephews came along and complicated the ever-loving hell out of my life. Now I'm going to Mommy and Me classes, One Direction concerts, the emergency room, and arguing cases in the principal's office.

Chelsea's too sweet, too innocent, and too gorgeous for her own good. She tries to be tough, but she's not. She needs someone to help her, defend her...and the kids.

And that—that, I know how to do.

*Appealed*

When Brent Mason looks at Kennedy Randolph, he doesn't see the awkward, sweet girl who grew up next door. He sees a self-assured, stunning woman...who wants to crush the most intimate--and prized--parts of his anatomy beneath the heels of her Louboutins.

When Kennedy looks at Brent, all she sees is the selfish, Abercrombie & Fitch catalogue-worthy teenager who humiliated her in high school in order to join the popular crowd. A crowd that made those years a living hell for her.

But she's not a lovesick social outcast anymore--she's a Washington, DC, prosecutor with a long winning streak. Brent is the opposing attorney in her next case, and Kennedy thinks it's time to put him through a little hell of his own.

But things aren't exactly working out the way she planned. Brent has his sights set on Kennedy, and every fiery exchange only makes him want her more--and makes her wonder if he's as passionate in the bedroom as he is in the courtroom. In the end, they may just find themselves in love...or in contempt of court.

33314331R00083

Made in the USA
San Bernardino, CA
30 April 2016